TURQUOISE MOUNTAIN

DIANE J. REED

Copyright © 2017 by Diane J. Reed
All rights reserved.
No part of this book may be reproduced in any form or by any electronic or mechanical means, including information storage and retrieval systems, without written permission from the author, except for the use of brief quotations in a book review.

Cover design by Najla Qamber at Najla Qamber Designs, www.najlaqamberdesigns.com

I

Dillon Iron Feather stood in the blue corner of the Octagon in silence, surrounded by a chain-link fence. His long, dark hair threaded over his broad shoulders, and he punched his gloves together, readying for the fight. With a few short jumps, he kept the adrenaline flowing that always made his reflexes lightning fast. Pausing to draw a deep breath, he bowed his head for a moment and began to mutter a low chant. Then he stroked a piece of turquoise he'd secretly sewn into the waistband of his shorts.

The old stone slowly grew warm.

The turquoise was thin enough that officials never detected it when they frisked him before a fight. But Dillon trusted in the gem the way medicine men rely on incantations for rain. It was a tradition among the Apache that *dáatł'įįí*, the treasured stone they believed could be found at the end of rainbows, helped improve a warrior's aim. This particular piece was an heirloom from Dillon's great-great grandfather Iron Feather, an expert tracker in the nineteenth century who moonlighted as a train robber. The only item the famous outlaw left his descendants was his medicine pouch filled with herbs and stones that were rumored to convey supernatural power. Three of those stones were turquoise and were handed down to Dillon and his brothers Barrett and Lander.

Dillon regarded himself as the keeper of the sacred pouch, the most valuable thing he owned. He rubbed the piece of turquoise one last time, then folded his large arms, riddled with muscle, and spread his legs into a fighter's stance. His nearly obsidian eyes gazed out over the Las Vegas crowd at the MGM Grand Garden Arena as though in a trance.

In his mind, Dillon was tracing his enemy's tracks.

Like his part-Apache ancestor before him, Dillon reviewed every possible move his opponent might make. He'd gleaned this information from watching endless pay-per-view bouts and scouring articles written about the man, studying him like prey. It wasn't hard to find media coverage on Butch Fowler, aka Baby Fat, the reigning middleweight mixed martial arts champion of the world. The guy hadn't lost a fight in eighteen months. Dillon had memorized Baby Fat's stats, knowing he'd earned his nickname by training like a demon on skimpy rations for months before a fight, then carb loading two weeks prior so there was a rubbery layer of fat over his entire frame that made him as slippery as hell. Only idiots were fooled by his round face and oddly plump demeanor. As an expert in Brazilian Jiu Jitsu, if Baby Fat managed to take you down to the mat, he'd coil you like a snake with his thick legs and do an Anaconda Choke around your neck that would have you tapping out and surrendering the match in seconds flat.

The crowds loved him for it.

And as Baby Fat ascended the stairs to take his place in the red corner of the Octagon, a stream of trash talk left his lips that made 17,000 people roar and stand to their feet. Baby Fat strutted around with his crimson mohawk sticking straight up like a rooster's comb and laughed, giving Dillon the finger. He never called out Dillon's name because frankly he couldn't remember it. This was simply an early-season fight with someone he expected to force into submission within the first round. The tall, Native American-looking man with a big frame and cheekbones that rivaled the cliffs of Mount Rushmore was known in cage fighting circles to move like a shadow, dark and quiet, a guy who never engaged in trash talk at all. A couple of announcers had made hay out of Dillon Iron Feather's last name, joking that he was a savage striker who could throw punches like tomahawks, but Baby Fat didn't care. The only thing that crossed the MMA veteran's mind was the six-figure deal he'd inked that morning with a sponsor to sell protein shakes on QVC.

So when the referee motioned for the two men to move to the center of the arena, repeated the standard rules, and told them to touch gloves, Baby Fat actually released a dramatic yawn. The crowd swelled with laughter.

"C'mon, girly-girl!" he taunted Dillon, pointing at his lush, long hair. "Let's get this over with."

A slight smile etched Dillon's lips. His gaze burned.

In a low voice, he chanted an old song just loud enough for Baby Fat to hear, an ancient Apache petition for success in battle. Dillon opened the fight by dancing warily around his opponent, then spinning into a Tae Kwon Do back kick aimed straight for Baby Fat's head. His opponent took the blow with the same detachment of a stiff punching bag, yet it forced him to keep his distance. Baby Fat scoffed loudly at Dillon like he was the one afraid to move closer, but he remained stoic when Dillon threw another kick to his knee—going for the fragile ACL on the leg he liked to lead on—which made him wince. Baby Fat retaliated with swings to the jaw, clipping Dillon once, but not before Dillon succeeded in spiking him in the gut. Without hesitating to catch his breath, Baby Fat dove for Dillon's waist in order to bring him down in one of his grapples on the mat that had made him famous. Dillon's knee was under Baby Fat's chin faster than he could blink, making his head snap back and his ears ring. Enraged, Baby Fat lunged for Dillon's face with haymakers that would have made most ordinary men see stars.

Dillon took the abuse like he was used to it, dipping and swaying to avoid more punches, but he struggled to stay conscious. Baby Fat's blows had the impact of wrecking balls, and he knew if he didn't dodge them better, the fight would be over in a heartbeat. Gathering his wits, he delivered a fierce uppercut to the side of Baby Fat's head that flattened him against the chain-link fence. The maneuver only made Baby Fat madder, and he targeted Dillon's gut again with a clinch to force a takedown. Another knee to Baby Fat's jaw prevented him from dropping the fight to the floor, and by now Baby Fat's face was bloody from Dillon's counter slams. He surged forward and hammered at Dillon, making him teeter badly. For a moment, Dillon stumbled back as if he were hearing a chorus of songbirds.

"How you like that, Injun?" Baby Fat called out while the

crowd thundered in adoration. "You're wasting my time! You got nothin' kid—go crawl back to your tribe." Baby Fat set his fists on his hips, mouth crinkling into a cocky smile as he stepped forward to drill Dillon's head, expecting him to fall like a sack of potatoes.

And that's where Baby Fat made his biggest mistake.

All at once, Baby Fat was no longer six feet of pure muscle and bone covered by far too many donuts. The same killing machine Dillon had been studying for months had completely evaporated. In his place stood a mere seventeen-year-old boy.

A particularly rangy, red-haired teen in torn jeans and cowboy boots who'd mocked Dillon exactly the same way at the Wilson Ranch for Wayward Boys in Colorado. It was the juvenile delinquent program where Dillon and his younger brothers Barrett and Lander had spent their miserable adolescence after their parents died in a car crash. This bully with the red hair and crooked grin had tormented the Iron Feather brothers every single day for a year, despite their grief, and relentlessly pounded fifteen-year-old Dillon into the dust each time he'd tried to defend them. Unfortunately, the bully had graduated from the Wilson Ranch before Dillon hit sixteen and had finally grown tall and strong enough to stop anyone from abusing them again.

Dillon had been fighting that boy's shadow ever since...

That is, until he saw the deep scorn that gleamed from Baby Fat's eyes—a familiar derision that had poisoned Dillon's soul for years. This time, he was no longer just going to fight.

Dillon was going to kill him.

Inside his waistband, while Dillon's face was taking blow

after blow from Baby Fat, the turquoise stone against his skin grew cold.

Colder than ice.

That's what no one ever mentions about the kind of rage that resigns itself to murder.

It doesn't burn hot, like anger. It's more vicious and calculating, as cold as the bottom of the ocean. And strangely empty of emotion even remotely close to human feeling.

Some of Dillon's relatives used to call it the Dark Cave—

The bottomless lair of Big *Yi'yee*, the legendary Apache monster who eats men.

Dillon called it justice.

As Baby Fat struggled to grab Dillon's neck to shove him down to the mat, Dillon blocked him and delivered a blow to the side of his jaw.

It wasn't just any blow.

Dillon seized his moment and poured every ounce of strength and hatred he had into mashing Baby Fat's jaw with a torque that could spin his brain inside his skull, knocking him out before he hit the floor.

Baby Fat dropped to the mat with a deep sound that reverberated through the Octagon like a felled column of stone.

He didn't get up.

He didn't tap out, either.

Nor did Baby Fat respond when the ref patted his cheeks and called out his name.

Instantly, a swarm of medics toting emergency equipment surrounded the veteran fighter while the arena remained eerily silent. Not even the shrill announcer dared to crow about the surprising turn of what was supposed to be an ordinary, early-season match. Minutes passed as Baby Fat lay prostrate on the mat, unresponsive to the medics' efforts.

"Is he knocked out? Or is Baby Fat...dead?" the announcer dared to whisper into his microphone.

Standing quietly in the blue corner of the Octagon, Dillon wasn't certain. All sound had ceased for him except for his heartbeat pounding in his ears like a giant hammer. His vision had blurred to the color of crimson from the stream of his own blood that trickled down his face. A singular voice broke through the silence.

"Dad! Dad—can you hear me? Daddy!"

Stunned, Dillon wiped his eyes and lifted his gaze from his opponent's body. He spied an auburn-haired teenage boy outside the ring who looked just like Baby Fat, his hands clinging desperately to the chain-link fence. Beside him was a blonde woman with her arm wrapped around his shoulder, her face pale in shock. Dillon recognized her—she was Baby Fat's wife. A leggy Las Vegas showgirl who had her own fitness reality show called *Fighting Fat* that occasionally featured cameos of her famous husband. The boy next to her stared at Dillon with a death face—the same anguished horror Dillon remembered all too well when he'd learned that his own parents had passed.

It was the look of loss.

The look of your whole world never being the same again.

The look of a childhood ending for good.

While the medics carefully loaded Baby Fat's large, motionless frame onto a gurney and strapped him down to rush him to an awaiting ambulance, Dillon wriggled out the turquoise stone from inside his waistband and cradled it in his palm like a chunk of ice.

The stone didn't warm to his body temperature.

Dillon pressed his hands together, rubbing furiously for a moment, but the turquoise remained cold.

In that moment, he knew only one thing:

His opponent would never bully anyone again—and his family would be destroyed forever.

And it was all because of Dillon.

2

"Faster!" the workshop manager yelled to the group of artisans in the small, dusty warehouse. "We have deadlines to make!"

Tessa rubbed her eyes, setting down her jeweler's tools with a sigh.

"Why do they have to be such jerks?" grumbled a woman at the work station next to her. "These are supposed to be one-of-a-kind designs. And now they're working us like a sweat shop?"

"I know," replied Tessa, squinting at the dirty windows that barely let in enough light. She tightened the elastic on her ponytail to keep her silky, long blonde hair from falling into her face. "When I first started here a year ago, I believed that line that we were creating art. It was exciting." She lowered her voice. "But I heard Arthur Jacquier cut a new deal with the rappers at Arrest Records to wear our designs at an awards show. Now he wants us to work double time. Crap, speak of the devil—"

"Good morning!" The skinny, middle-aged man slid next to Tessa, standing so close he could kiss her. The chunky gold necklace he wore with a ruby pendant in a heavy setting hardly matched his pale skin and tailored herringbone suit, but he held it up with pride anyway. "How's my favorite designer this morning, Number One?"

Tessa winced, inching away from him.

Everyone who worked at Jacquier & Co., Arthur's jewelry company, was forced to use a designer's number from the day they were hired. It was a safeguard measure, he explained, so no one could claim individual credit for designs he professed were a "group effort." But after working there a year, Tessa had learned the real reason: It was to prevent talented people like her, who poured her soul into her creations, from ever becoming famous in her own right. And now Arthur took credit for everything she made—regardless of the fact that she was his top designer.

Oh, to be young with stars in your eyes in New York, she thought.

At twenty-five, Tessa didn't have many choices for jobs last year after taking care of her single mother until her death from cancer. She'd put herself through art school and paid her mother's bills by driving a taxi, and she'd seen it all—sex in the back seat, jerks who tried to sell drugs from cab windows, even gunshots. Her life was enough to make her flop on the couch each night and watch *Bonanza* reruns with a carton of Häagen-Dazs, dreaming of living in a simpler place with wide open spaces. A land without blaring horns or pimps and pushers on every corner. A land where she'd want to stay.

But how could she ever find such a place without a decent job? Tessa didn't have a trust fund, like many of her colleagues at art school, and her heart craved creativity beyond the monotony of driving a taxi. So after graduation when she'd aced the interview at Jacquier & Co. with her award-winning silver designs, she jumped at the chance to put her imagination to work making jewelry for hot rappers and A-list film stars.

Now, all she could think about was how to make her escape.

"Mail call, my lovelies!" Arthur trilled, holding up a stack of mail and a brown-paper wrapped package.

Tessa dug her fingers into her skirt, resisting the urge to smack him.

He always acted like the designers were his harem—all of which were female, a fact she hadn't been allowed to observe until after she'd started working there. What made things worse was that Arthur brazenly rifled through everyone's mail to make sure they didn't get offers from other firms, because God knows they weren't allowed to have email accounts at work—or computers, for that matter. Shaking her head, Tessa waited for him to hand over whatever junk mail was in his stack as his excuse to interact with her. It was no secret Arthur was desperate for her attention, and word around the water cooler claimed he thought Tessa had the "hottest body".

Arthur flashed her a smile, and to her surprise, placed a brown package on top of a magazine into her hands.

"I hope that box doesn't contain any business correspondence," he shot her a warning look. "Don't forget my office window on the second floor. I see everything you do." He trailed his gaze along her ample curves that she'd tried to hide under a frumpy sweater and skirt. "And I mean *everything*, my Number One."

Tessa wanted to throw up.

She'd learned to despise that term, so she gently disguised the number she was forced to stamp on all her designs. Instead of a mere digit next to the company logo, she always placed a delicate, vertical image that was frayed at the edges, looking more like a feather than a number. This tiny act of rebellion gave her hope every time. The feather design had come to her once in a dream, and she never forgot the way she felt when she woke up that morning. Rather than groan at having to go to work again under Arthur's constant stare, she felt…

Free.

Like wings had been attached to her heart.

And if she could only muster enough faith, they might lead her to a horizon where her talents could really blossom. Not just to another exploitive job in a big city. But to a place that she could call…

Home.

Home to her soul. To her creativity. To the song in her heart that had always longed to be sung through her unique designs.

That home wasn't exactly in this musty old warehouse in New York creating heavy jewelry with enough carats to make celebrities sparkle brighter than the paparazzi's flashbulbs.

"Wake up, sleepyhead!" Arthur chided, jiggling Tessa's shoulder to interrupt the daydreamy look in her eyes before he returned to his office. "We got a batch of blue topaz from

Texas today that I want you to set before the rappers' award show in two weeks. I'm counting on you to be brilliant again!"

"Right," Tessa mumbled. "Brilliant."

Brushing stray hairs from her face, she sat down for a moment to open a chocolate-chip granola bar and check out her mail. She flipped through the jewelry trade magazine and set it aside, her gaze settling on the brown package. Curious, she ripped apart the paper.

Tessa sucked in a deep breath—

Inside the wrapper was an old cigar box. It was chipped at the edges with a faded green label across the front.

Stunned, Tessa recognized that box.

It had belonged to her grandfather in Colorado. She'd gone with her mother to visit him one summer when she was ten. He was a crotchety man, living alone in a rusty trailer way up in the mountains. Her mother said he'd gone off kilter ever since Grandma had passed, and he was convinced he could prospect for gold. Yet he seemed to delight in his young granddaughter, letting her sleep on his trailer floor and cooking her favorite stew and biscuits at night, then taking her out into the wilderness during the day. Tessa was in total heaven, giddy with the freedom she'd had to explore the majestic beauty of the backcountry, and it was then that she'd fallen in love with the West. The towering mountains, verdant trees, and open spaces encouraged her to hear the whispers of her heart. In the evenings, her grandfather made a special point of showing her his cigar box. He said it belonged to his own grandfather who lived in the nineteenth century.

Hesitantly, Tessa pried open the weathered box, ignoring the commands of Jacquier's floor manager to keep busy.

Among old screws, nails, and pieces of scrap leather was a long feather. White, with bands of grey, that had once belonged to a great horned owl.

But it wasn't an ordinary feather.

Tessa's grandfather had told her it came from a famous train robber in the nineteenth century who ran with the Bandits Hollow Gang. His name was Iron Feather, and legend claimed that Tessa's great-great-grandfather had helped him and his gang hide once from a posse in hot pursuit. In return, he gave him this simple feather.

It was supposed to be capable of magic…

Tessa smiled, recalling how her grandfather played on her girlish imagination and told her all kinds of stories. Including the idea that Iron Feather had a familiar in the form of an owl who watched over him and his descendants to this day because of their ancestor's kind deed. Her eyebrows knit together, however, when she spied an envelope beneath the feather in the cigar box. Gently, she opened the seal and pulled out a letter:

Dear Theresa Grove,

We apologize for sending this message to you at your place of employment, but we were unable to locate your current address. We are writing to inform you that your grandfather, Benjamin Grove IV, has passed away, and he specifically stated in his will that he bequeathed his cigar box to you. It appears to be of little value, yet out of respect for your relative's wishes, we have taken the trouble to forward this package to you. May your memories bring you peace during this difficult time of transition.

It was signed by a law firm in Colorado. Tessa's eyes became misty, wishing she could have visited her grandfather more, and she picked up the feather and stroked it, feeling tingles chase down her spine. Beside an old battery and some faded baseball cards in the cigar box, she spotted a piece of paper with the words *Mining Claim* at the top.

Tessa set down the feather.

Mining claim?

She knew her grandfather liked to look for gold. She peered at the certificate more closely. It gave the section coordinates for a specific parcel in Bandits Hollow, Colorado, about a quarter of an acre, and granted all mining rights to any precious metals or minerals therein. The expiration date was six months from now.

Stapled to it was the original mining claim staked out in 1895, along with an old map to its whereabouts. The claim had been issued to Benjamin Grove I.

Tessa's heart began to race.

That was the name of her ancestor who'd helped Iron Feather. This mining claim had been in her family for generations. Over a hundred years…

There must have been a reason.

Tessa glanced at the thin pieces of gold and silver that were scattered around her work station from all the rings and necklaces she'd made.

Colorado was famous for its reserves of gold, silver, and copper. She knew the very same remnants of gold she was staring at came from a mine in that state. So where on earth was Bandits Hollow?

Quickly, she typed the name of the town into her cell

phone app and watched a map loom large on her screen. Bandits Hollow appeared to be about fifteen miles north of Cripple Creek, a famous gold region, surrounded by national forest.

Tessa's heart throbbed harder.

So there *could* be something there—precious gems or metals. Wasn't Colorado renowned for aquamarine, garnet, and topaz, as well as silver and gold? Tessa knew her sources like the back of her hand, because Jacquier & Co.'s customers insisted on American stones whenever they could get them. Bandits Hollow was clearly within a well-known mining district, and a lot of gems were found near the same places as gold. What were the odds that *she* could find something there?

Then I wouldn't have to be anyone's worker bee anymore, Tessa thought. I'd have a fresh supply of gems or metals and be able to open my own business. Nervous, she paused to mull over the possibilities. Boutiques in Aspen and Vail regularly scooped up the wares she'd created for Jacquier & Co., demanding more before she could even finish the original orders. All at once, it dawned on her that nothing was stopping her from selling her designs to these high-end Colorado retailers *herself*.

Tessa cast a quick glance at her harried coworkers in the warehouse, most of whom were around her age, yet looked a decade older in the dim light as they soldered with crimped fingers and beads of perspiration over their brows. Hesitantly, she steered her gaze to the second floor. Sure enough, there was Arthur standing outside his office with his arms crossed, tapping his foot while staring down at her in disapproval.

Do you really want to be trapped under that bully's gaze,

she asked herself, known only as a number for the rest of your career? When you could hot foot it to Colorado and strike out on your own?

Wild notions flooded her mind, overriding the picture she'd always had of herself as methodical and responsible. The one who took care of her mother during her long illness, who always paid the bills and never did anything spontaneous. And who was going to grow old and fade into this warehouse's cobwebs if she didn't change her life strategy soon—

Oh my God, Tessa wondered, have I gone off-the-charts crazy?

She picked up the feather again, twirling it nervously between her fingers. All at once, a rush of tingles skipped through her hand and up her arm, pooling in the center of her chest as if her heart were on fire. The warehouse became hazy and disappeared. All Tessa could see before her were rugged mountains and a beautiful green meadow, with a wide blue sky that stretched into infinity. She gasped at the apparition, yet she couldn't stop herself from lifting the feather in her hand to trace *Tessa Grove Designs* in a wispy, cloud-like script across the horizon, as though it might actually make her dream come true.

"That's always been my goal," she admitted under her breath, "to own my own company." Curiously, the longer she held the feather in her hand, the bolder and more courageous her thoughts became, as if the feather heard her and somehow magnified her hopes. You know, she recalled, the lease on my apartment *does* run out at the end of the month—I can get my full deposit back. And I have a ten-thousand-dollar credit limit on my MasterCard. That's enough to live on for several months. I've got polishing tools and an entire stock of silver from my days at art school. If the mine has *anything* of value—even agates or jasper—I could make plenty of items to take to exclusive boutiques in Colorado to show off my work. I could completely...

Start over.

Goosebumps danced across Tessa's skin. Isn't that what I've always wanted, she thought, to create heirloom designs that feed the soul? To do more than fashion heavy bling for a bunch of celebrities who'll never even know my name? She clutched her fingers tightly around the owl feather as though it imparted supernatural strength. What if this is my one shot to make my dream come true? she pondered. I'm only twenty-five—I have the whole rest of my life to be merely a number for somebody else if I fail.

"My Number One!" Arthur startled Tessa by digging his hand into her elbow. His abrupt words made her mountain vision shatter, restoring the grim contours of the warehouse. With a painful grip, he jerked her from her chair and yanked forcefully on her arm until she rose to her feet. Staring into her wide, blue-green eyes, Arthur pressed his finger beneath her chin and turned her to face him.

"You're *not* staying on task," he barked. "What could possibly be in your mail that interests you so much? We're on deadline—"

"I-I know!" Tessa backpedaled, tucking the mining claim behind her where Arthur couldn't see. She gripped the quill of the feather like a lifeline. "I was, um, getting ready to start soldering."

Arthur scanned her work station with his brow raised at

the old cigar box filled with junk. "Looks like you were dawdling to me. As a matter of fact, I timed you." He tapped his sapphire-crusted watch with his logo on it. "You've been doing nothing but daydreaming for the last thirty minutes. I'll have to cut your pay."

He pulled her closer to him like she was something he owned, not a professional employee. Tessa flinched and attempted to back away, but he held her arm firm.

"Then again, if you want to make up your wasted time, you could stay late tonight for a personal design session." Arthur licked his lips. He carefully readjusted his gold cufflinks at his sleeves as if already imagining how his shirt might look on her, unbuttoned to her cleavage. "We can meet in my office and, um, chat about your newest ideas. If I like what I see," his eyes roamed over the fullness of her breasts and hips, "your paycheck might not have to reflect today's lapse."

He glanced past Tessa at a framed poster of Marilyn Monroe by the old warehouse clock on the wall. The iconic actress with tousled hair, similar to Tessa's pale color, was smiling and dripping in diamonds. Arthur nodded at the image. "Has anyone ever told you your figure's reminiscent of old Hollywood?" he whispered. "Curves like that should be draped in jewels." He traced a finger down her sweater. "It's such a shame you hide under that ugly cardigan."

He picked up a ruby cabochon from her desk, each facet reflecting the light so that it appeared to be on fire. He held it up to Tessa.

"This does match the color of your lips, doesn't it?" He leaned beside her ear. "I'd love to see how it looks against your skin."

Heat exploded against Tessa's cheeks as her blood boiled. Shaking her head, she couldn't tolerate Arthur's abuse one more minute. Sparks ignited on her fingers where she held the feather in her hand, making her feel more daring than she had in her whole life. With a swiftness that surprised her, she snatched the ruby cabochon away from Arthur's grip and set it down on her work station with a hard clink.

Then she hauled off and slapped him.

"I have a name, goddammit! It's Tessa Grove. And I am *not* your Number One."

The warehouse fell silent. The other artisans had ceased their soldering and polishing and turned to stare at Tessa and Arthur in wonder. In the dead silence, she heard a coworker whisper, "You go, girl!"

"Now, now," Arthur responded loudly so everyone could hear. "There's plenty of more artists where you came from. Face it, you're a dime a dozen in New York. You wouldn't want me to fire you for insubordination, would you—"

"Do whatever the hell you want." Tessa grabbed her purse and slipped the mining claim and feather inside, then seized her grandfather's cigar box. "Because I quit."

"You're joking—we're on deadline! Believe me, I'll make certain you never get a job with another jeweler in this city again—"

"I won't need one," Tessa stated flatly.

"What do you mean? Where are you going—"

Her lips curled into a smile as a crazy, new-found confidence surged through her veins. She couldn't explain it, but with the owl feather in her purse, she felt as if she'd been handed her wings. Squaring her shoulders, Tessa broke free from her work station and marched toward the front door. When she reached the exit, she flung the door open wide and turned to face Arthur.

"I am going precisely to where you'll never find me," she promised him. "So don't even try."

3

Tessa clung for dear life onto the door handle of the beat-up truck, wondering if she'd lost her mind. Apparently in this part of Colorado, a rusty '48 Ford carrying a load of hay was their idea of a "taxi." She'd taken the bus forty minutes north from the Colorado Springs Airport, then called the number she'd found in the local *Nickel Ads* sitting on a bench at the bus stop for Dusty's Cab Service.

"This is great!" Dusty remarked as he steered his vintage red pickup along the tight bend in the mountain road. "I have to deliver hay to the Lazy C Ranch anyway. So I'll drop you off at Bandits Hollow before I unload. You staying at the Golden Wagon Hotel? Nell runs a mighty fine place, and she's got a nice restaurant, too. Tell her Dusty sent ya."

"Um, well, I was hoping we could make a stop before we actually get to Bandits Hollow." Tessa rifled through her purse and handed Dusty the old map to her mining claim.

"What the hell?" Dusty pulled over to a turn-out by the side of the road and brought his truck to a stop. He squinted to make out the directions. "Lady, that location is over by Outlaw Pass." He flicked his hand in the vague direction of a mountain range dusted with snow. "You need a four-wheel drive to go up those roads. You prospecting for gold or something? I gotta tell you, a lot of those old mines ain't safe to poke around. They can fall in on you without so much as a warning."

Tessa sighed and gazed at the radiant aspens spread like golden quilt patches over the mountains. It was early October, and the Rocky Mountains at high elevation were spectacular with color. Amber and vermillion leaves shivered on the trees that lined the road, and Tessa was grateful the beauty of the landscape echoed her childhood memories, making the trip worth it. Yet her chest tightened when she turned to answer Dusty, wondering if his sense of direction might lead down some precipitous backroad that would leave them forever lost.

"That mine used to be my grandfather's claim," Tessa explained. "I want to see it before nightfall. Do you think you can find it?"

"Ain't guaranteeing nothin'." Dusty shook his head, continuing up the road. "I can give the route a go, but if we come across a washout or a felled tree, I'm turning right back around. My cell phone service don't work out here, and unless you happen to have a winch in your suitcase and a buddy with a four-by-four to pull us out, I don't aim to get stuck any time soon."

"Deal," Tessa nodded.

She braced herself as Dusty turned down a dirt lane that led higher into the mountains, cutting across slopes with steep drop offs. The precarious shelf road became rockier the farther they went, jostling the truck to the point that Tessa felt like she'd crawled inside a washing machine. Occasionally a hay bale fell off the truck bed, and Dusty had to get out and throw it back on. Each time he climbed behind the wheel again with a smile.

"How do you like off roading?" He finally chuckled. "Kinda fun, ain't it?"

Tessa shrugged. If she hadn't visited her grandfather when she was ten and toured the backcountry in his relic of a Jeep held together by wire and spare parts, she probably would have been petrified. Even so, she wasn't exactly comfortable with this form of travel, but she knew it went with the territory.

Dusty slowed the truck to a crawl to make it through a dried-out ravine, nearly tumbling another bale off the back. After several more miles of steep grades that climbed up and down, rutted in the middle by old creek beds that he had to straddle with his truck wheels, Dusty pointed to a thin dirt lane that veered left from their route. "Over there is where that mine's supposed to be," he claimed. "So far we got lucky with no boulders in the way. And if I read your map right, it should only be another half mile." He lifted his visor and tracked the position of the late afternoon sun. "There should be enough light out to see your mine before we head over to Bandits Hollow. Hold on!"

Dusty gunned the truck to make it up a sharp rise,

dropping a few more bales before reaching the next road. "Don't worry, I'll get 'em on the way back!" he assured Tessa. After a few minutes, the pines and aspens cleared and the road snaked through a beautiful, high mountain meadow replete with lush grass that looked like a green carpet stretching out before them. On the opposite side of the meadow was an old barn with a corral. A log cabin sat beside it, its weathered wood beams glowing a rich brown with glints of amber in the late afternoon light. When Tessa turned and spied a grassy knoll near the cabin with a rustic door wedged into it, she gasped.

"There's your mine on that hill." Dusty high-fived Tessa. "We made it! Well I'll be darned—I didn't think this ol' truck had it in her."

Dusty coasted through the meadow toward the old buildings and the mine, stopping when they reached a gate marked by a giant timber frame. At the top nailed into a thick log was a sign burnt by branding-iron letters that said *Bandits Ranch*. Before Dusty could hop out to open the gate, a tall man stepped out of the old cabin. His massive frame filled the small porch. He looked fairly young, around Tessa's age, with long, dark hair that swept past his shoulders. Tessa's jaw dropped when she noticed he had no shirt on. The play of the late-afternoon sun across his bare chest highlighted the tan hue of his skin and deeply contoured muscles, each stretched tight like the very picture of a seasoned athlete. But what struck her most was the rugged, Native American features of his face. He stood on the porch of the cabin and folded his thick arms that were large enough to crush anyone who ventured near. Then he scanned the intruders with a steel expression as though he were a tribal leader contemplating war.

"Holy shit!" exclaimed Dusty. "Th-that's the guy. In the fight—"

"What? What are you talking about?" Tessa shook Dusty's shoulder. "You know him?"

"Are you kidding? He's a fricking rock star! He came from nowhere and took out the middleweight champion of the world in a cage fight last year. The most famous fight in history. That man's a killer."

"Killer? As in, his opponent's…dead?"

"Last I heard."

"Great! So what's he doing on my land?" Tessa pressed.

Dusty shook his head, and Tessa grew impatient with the long tree shadows that had begun to stretch over the meadow, indicating the sun was going to set soon. It didn't help matters that the man on the porch was so breathtakingly gorgeous she found herself staring at him again like an idiot, unable to move to a muscle.

"O-Okay," she offered, attempting to snap out of her stupor, "I'll try talking to him for a minute. Maybe he's some kind of caretaker for this property, and he doesn't know my grandfather died. After all, his trailer was in another county." She hopped out of the truck and walked up to the gate to unclasp the latch, swinging it open. With a little hesitation, Dusty drove forward a few yards and waited for her.

"Hello there!" Tessa called out to the tall stranger, determined not to be distracted by his formidable good looks. She managed a cheerful wave. "Hello?"

He made no reply.

Nor did he bother to move.

He simply stood his ground on the porch, glaring at her intently.

Tessa inched a bit closer, realizing he had to be over six feet tall with the way he towered over the porch. He was quite intimidating, with broad shoulders and biceps so firm you could bounce quarters off them. And then there was that face —deep brown eyes outlined by high cheekbones and a jaw that could carve stone. Good grief, she confided to herself, he looks like the kind of movie handsome that just stepped out of some western film. I've got to stay focused—gawking at a stranger is *not* what I came here for.

Nevertheless, Tessa's quiet observations from a respectful distance didn't exactly soften the hard look in the man's eyes. Her stomach began to fill with anxious butterflies. "I, um… I'm Tessa Grove," she introduced herself, pointing to the rustic door on the nearby hill. "I've come all the way from New York to see that mine over there." She reached into her purse and pulled out the mining claim and the map she'd retrieved from Dusty, holding them up like white flags.

"See? I wanted to take a look at it today. Do you mind if I ask your name and what you're doing on my property?"

Rather than answer, the man turned and disappeared into the cabin.

Tessa threw up her hands. "Swell!" she grumbled. "Now he's decided to be shy. And we're running out of light soon. Guess I'll head over to the mine myself and peek inside."

After taking a few strides, she saw the man reappear at the entrance of the cabin.

Only this time, he had a shotgun.

"Whoa, hold on!" Tessa piped up. "I've got a legal right to be here—"

The man pumped his weapon and aimed straight for Dusty's truck. He fired, shattering a side mirror into a million pieces.

Faster than Tessa could call out "run for your life," Dusty had already spun the truck around, bales flying, and hightailed it down the road. Clouds of dirt erupted from his tires.

"Wait!" Tessa shouted. "Y-You've got my luggage!"

She dashed after the truck, dodging hay bales and sprigs of alfalfa, feeling like a fool for reaching out her arms as if she could actually snag a ride on the back of a speeding pickup. Coughing, she tried to remember the right way back to the main road and thanked God she'd worn sneakers. Then she heard another blast from the man's gun and ducked, praying she wouldn't get a hole blown into her back. Falling to her knees, she crawled over the uneven road, bruising her legs on the hard rocks, when she felt a large hand grab her by the arm and lift her to her feet.

Tessa was face to face with the dangerous stranger from the cabin. His dark eyes bored into hers.

"You're trespassing," he stated in a deep voice. His mouth became a firm line.

"No, I'm not," Tessa spit out, hacking from dust. By God, she'd finally worked up the guts to stand up to Arthur Jacquier only two weeks ago, and she wasn't about to start backing down in her life now. Gun or no gun, she was going contend for what was hers—even if it meant facing this backwoods whack job and his weapon.

Tessa elbowed him hard, like she'd learned in a New York

City defense class, and sank her teeth into his hand on her arm until she managed to yank herself free.

"I'm *not* trespassing!" She stepped back, ready to duck if he tried to swing that shotgun at her. She stared him square in the eye and pointed her finger into his face. "You are!"

4

The man grabbed the mining claim and map from Tessa's hand. His dark eyes creased as he scanned the details. "This *isn't* your property. And something tells me your name isn't Benjamin Grove the Fourth—"

"He was my grandfather. I'm Tessa Grove, like I said, and he passed away and left the claim to me. It doesn't expire for another six months, which means I have legal title to that mine."

"You only have mineral rights to a hole in the ground." He nodded in the direction of the mine. "Which means you can't set foot on my property."

"What?" Tessa crossed her arms.

"You heard me. This piece of paper entitles you to dig behind that old wooden door. That's all. And my land surrounds every inch of it. Which means you're breaking the law by getting anywhere near that mine. So get lost."

"Wait, you can't deny access to what's legally mine!"

"Can't I?" His face broke into a wry smile. For a moment, his eyes sparkled at the prospect of challenge, lighting them up to a warm, charming brown.

Damn! Tessa cursed to herself. *That's all I need right now is a guy who gets more good looking when he taunts me—*

Fuming, she boldly yanked the mining claim and map from his hand to scrutinize them. According to her documents, it looked like her ancestor was the one who originally built Grove Road that led to this mining parcel, which sat right smack dab on the stranger's property. Okay, so he was right—her quarter acre didn't include any of his buildings, but it connected to the road. And nowhere did it specify that she was required to get permission from any stranger to use that dirt lane. But how could she convince him of that?

"Listen," Tessa sighed, "I know it might seem out of the blue that I'm here. But my grandfather meant a lot to me. And this place—this gold mine—it's…it's kind of sacred. What I mean is, my great-great-grandfather found it only because a Native American outlaw gave him some powerful medicine. That might sound crazy to you, but it's true. His name was Iron Feather—"

"Your great-great grandfather *knew* Iron Feather?"

Tessa nodded. "He was Benjamin Grove the First, and he helped Iron Feather and the Bandits Hollow Gang hide from a posse." She dug into her purse and held up the sacred owl feather. "All Iron Feather had to give him in return was this, but it was rumored to have, you know—"

"Special powers."

To Tessa's amazement, the stranger's face darkened in thought. He studied the feather for a long time as though it were a precious artifact. Then he looked out over the mountain tops at the threads of garnet in the sky that had begun to spread from the dipping sun. His eyes seemed very far away.

It's the feather, Tessa realized. He knows something about that feather…

The man returned his gaze to Tessa. Yet when he reached for the feather, she seized her moment and surprised him by lunging for his shotgun. She managed to grab it and run several strides, when she whipped around.

"Back off, whoever you are!" She aimed the shotgun straight at him and pumped it awkwardly, barely remembering how from when her grandfather taught her fifteen years ago. "I want to see that mine," she demanded, her body visibly trembling. "And I'm not leaving till I do."

The man smirked, his gaze tracing her wild blonde hair that had fallen across her face, her blue-green eyes spitting fury. What Tessa hadn't noticed in her panic, of course, was that her purse had fallen from her shoulder and spilled onto the ground. He crouched carefully to the grass, keeping his eye firmly on the gun barrel, and picked up some of the contents before standing to his feet.

"Where do you expect to go after this if I've got your ID and credit cards, city girl?" He smiled, noticing the blush that suffused her cheeks. Her eyes darted to the drivers license and MasterCard he held in his hand, and that was all the opening he needed. With an expertly aimed kick, he knocked the shotgun from her grip and sent it twirling in air, then caught it. He set the butt down on the ground.

"You should know your opponent a whole lot better before

you start a fight," he scolded. "Now you don't have your purse or a weapon. Fortunately, you're far too pretty for shooting practice today. But don't press your luck."

Another blush warmed Tessa's cheeks, and she cradled her arms tight to try and stop the tremors. To her astonishment, the man threw down his gun and caught up to her within a couple of strides. Before she knew it, she was born aloft by the stranger's strong arms, her body next to his warm, hard chest. Despite her kicks and screams, he set her gently on the grass and pulled a long piece of baling twine from his pocket, then proceeded to tie up her hands and feet.

"What the hell are you doing!" Tessa screamed, wriggling on the grass like an angry caterpillar. "First you threatened me with a gun, and now kidnapping? You're going to face the law for this!"

"For your information, lady, I deliberately shot out the truck mirror and fired the second shot in the air to scare you off. I have no intention of killing anybody today. But I will make sure you have a soft bed and a good meal in your belly, since you appear to be stranded, no matter how hot headed you are."

With that, he pulled a bandana from his pocket and stuffed it in Tessa's mouth. She kept thrashing violently while he picked up the scattered items on the meadow and returned them along with her ID and credit card to her purse.

But he slipped the owl feather into his pocket.

Just then, Tessa saw vivid red and blue lights trace over the cabin and barn as the shrill sound of a siren echoed off the hillsides. A police cruiser appeared at the front gate, and an officer stepped out.

"Dammit, Dillon!" The officer called out. "What have you done to this poor woman? For crying out loud, are you that desperate for female company?" He walked boldly toward them. "Good thing Dusty went to the Lazy C Ranch and called 911."

Dillon laughed. "As a matter of fact, Barrett," he replied, picking up Tessa's squirming body and heading toward the cruiser, "I was about to bring her to you anyway. She's lost, and if she hadn't been so pig-headed about refusing to leave, I would have driven her to Bandits Hollow myself without hog-tying her."

Dillon set Tessa to a standing position beside the car and opened the door. Then he scooped her up again in his arms and hesitated for a moment, as though enjoying the feel of her curvaceous body against his broad chest. His lips turned up at the edges when he saw the rage in her expression as she wriggled relentlessly, indicating she wasn't about to quit fighting any time soon. Carefully, he laid her down across the back seat. Brushing aside a wild lock of hair from her face, he paused as though struck by the color of her piercing, blue-green eyes.

"Here," he said, turning to Barrett, "this is a hundred bucks." He gave him a wad of crinkled bills from his pocket. "That ought to put her up at the Golden Wagon Hotel and buy her a few meals. If she needs to stay a little longer, tell Nell to bill me. But don't you dare drop her off at my place again."

Barrett shook his head. "Ever the gentleman, Dillon," he rolled his eyes, "in your twisted kind of way. No wonder you're single! If people only knew what a sucker you are for a pretty woman, it would quiet at least half the rumors about you in this town."

"Who wants to quiet the rumors?" Dillon hung his thumbs off the front pockets of his jeans. "At least it keeps the riff raff away."

He snuck one last peek into Barrett's car, eyeing the way Tessa bucked and twisted on the back seat like a Mexican jumping bean, her cheeks beet red from attempting to scream. She shot him an angry glare. Another hint of a smile lifted the corners of Dillon's mouth, lingering in admiration.

"But I do have to say," he mentioned to Barrett, "that woman's nothing if not stubborn. And pretty damned gutsy for a New York city girl."

5

Tessa sat in the back of the police cruiser, rubbing the red welts on her wrists from where the officer had cut off the baling twine. She couldn't help noticing that Barrett's hair was as dark and thick as Dillon's, only cut short. And they were both tall with strong features and chiseled jawlines. She'd been too distracted in the frenzy of Dillon's tactics to try and read Barrett's badge when she got stuffed in the back seat. Yet with the way they looked so similar, she had to wonder…

"I assume you've guessed by now that Dillon and I are brothers," Barrett said, checking her reaction in his rear-view mirror. "And yes, he does have a point that you were trespassing."

"But I have a mining claim and rights to Grove Road!" Tessa countered. "I shouldn't have to be dropped by helicopter into a psychopath's backyard in order to see my mine."

Barrett laughed. "Yeah, I'm with you on the psychopath

part. Dillon's always been, uh, intense. Just so you know, he wan't going to hurt you."

"How can you say that? You weren't there," Tessa's voice shook with a frustrated edge. "He came at me with a shotgun and then tied me up!"

Barrett's eyes grew darker. "Because if he'd wanted to kill you, sweetheart, he would have done so by now. A man with his skills doesn't require a gun."

All attempts at words stifled in Tessa's throat.

"Take that as a compliment," Barrett noted. "He was enjoying your company in his own strange way. It's not every day he gets to spar with a lovely blonde who wandered into his remote neck of the woods."

Warmth prickled Tessa's cheeks. "Well if that's your brother's idea of flirting," she managed to hiss, "he needs serious therapy."

"Roger that," Barrett said. "You'd hardly be the first to suggest it. But I suspect there isn't an anger management expert on earth who could survive Dillon Iron Feather."

He steered the cruiser over a ridge that overlooked the twinkling lights of a small town on a hill at dusk. They passed by a road sign that said *Bandits Hollow, elevation 9,000 feet, population 150*.

"The Golden Wagon Hotel is up ahead," Barrett pointed out. "And I have explicit instructions to get you a room, free of charge."

"Keep the cash. I can pay for myself."

"No way," Barrett contended. "I'm not going to answer to Dillon for not putting you up. Have you seen his Tae Kwon Do back kick lately? I've been on the wrong end of that before and ended up in the hospital. Take the offer, and I promise I won't let him press charges for trespassing."

Tessa shook her head. These Iron Feather brothers are something else, she thought. But there was one thing she refused to let them railroad her on.

"I want my feather back," Tessa insisted.

"Feather? What feather?"

"The one your great-great grandfather gave mine. Dillon stole it after he tied me up. That's got to be against the law, or karma, or something."

The way Barrett's eyes gazed into the rearview mirror at Tessa took on a whole new dimension. "Y-Your family was connected to Iron Feather?"

"Damn straight," said Tessa. "How do you think I got that mine on Dillon's property? And if you men have any honor at all, you'll give me that feather back."

When Barrett finally parked his cruiser in Bandits Hollow, Tessa gazed out the window and blinked, doing a double take. Though the small town was draped in shadows from the early twilight hour, it was utterly charming, filled with the kind of historic storefronts and wooden boardwalks seen in period films of the old West. Toward the center of town, lit by old-fashioned street lamps, was a quaint gazebo in the middle of a park with a stage nearby, the kind used for weekend festivals. Beyond the park was an arena and several corrals with an *Outlaw Days Rodeo* sign hanging from a grandstand. Despite her fatigue, Tessa craned her neck to look up and down Main Street, her heart thrilling at the classic western architecture with bold colors and Victorian flourishes on buildings like the General Mercantile, the Miners Exchange, and the Old Colorado Bank, so different from the grubby warehouse district she'd left in New York. But it wasn't until Barrett opened the car door and escorted her from his cruiser to the Golden Wagon Hotel that her eyes grew really wide. In front of the hotel was an authentic nineteenth-century stagecoach painted from top to bottom in shimmering gold. And as Barrett grabbed the handle of the hotel door to swing it wide and usher her inside, Tessa stepped across the parquet wood floor of the lobby in awe. Before her was a broad staircase leading to the second floor flanked by marble columns. Velvet-patterned wallpaper lined the walls with occasional longhorn accents and vintage rodeo posters, making her feel like she'd slipped back in time.

"Well, howdy Barrett!" called out a slim, red-haired woman at the reception desk. She wore a yellow, Victorian dress with the word *Kit* on her name tag. "What brings you in here?"

"My brother Dillon," he sniffed with a surly look. "I'm under strict orders to get this little lady a meal and put her up for the night—on *his* dime." He strode confidently up to the woman and dug into his pocket, slapping the wad of bills on the desk. "What happens in Bandits Hollow stays in Bandits Hollow, right? Ain't no business of mine what she does after this, so long as she doesn't break the law." He turned to glare at Tessa. "I highly suggest you *don't* cross Dillon's path again, unless you want more trouble. Remember, I already bailed you out once."

"Wait," Tessa protested, "you can't keep me from my mine by shuffling me off to some hotel! Aren't you the law? I have legal title to that claim, even if it *is* on Dillon's property. And I'll be damned if I'll let the Iron Feather brothers push me aside or try to pay my bills. Listen, you haven't heard the last of Tessa Grove—"

"Suit yourself, ma'am," Barrett cut her off as he swiveled to walk away. "My part's done here, and duty calls. See you Friday morning, Kit." He gave the woman a casual wave as he headed to the door. "For the biscuits and gravy special."

Tessa's hands balled into fists while she watched Barrett saunter out the lobby. When she faced Kit, she knew her cheeks must be inflamed, but she couldn't help it. "God damn those Iron Feather brothers," she cursed under her breath. "They've done nothing but raise my blood pressure to the boiling point today every time I interacted with them."

"Aw, sweetheart," Kit gave her a kindly pat on the arm. "You're hardly the first person to say that. And you probably won't be the last."

"Well one thing's for sure," Tessa sighed, gazing at the bills on the desk. "I'd rather be dead than accept Dillon's money, no matter how much I need to save right now. Gives me the creeps just looking at it." She glanced up at Kit. "Would you, um, consider doing me a favor?"

"Waitress!" bellowed a man from inside the restaurant in the next room. He held up a mug. "My coffee's cold. When are you getting over here with a warm up?"

Kit's eyes grew frantic. "I'm sorry. Can you hold on a sec?" she implored Tessa. "I promise I'll be right back—"

She scurried into the restaurant to fill coffees at four

different booths by herself. Tessa watched while Kit wrote down a few orders from customers on a tablet and dashed across the room to give it to the cook. As fast as she could muster, she returned to the reception desk in the lobby, panting for breath.

"My apologies," she gasped. "Both Lila and Jenny are sick tonight, and we're shorthanded. Especially with Nell, the owner, out of town, and no one here to man the lobby. Lord, I don't know what we're gonna do. The Cattlemen Association's banquet is in an hour, and I'm the only one around. Oh," Kit suddenly appeared more flustered, staring at the wad of bills on the desk, "wasn't there something you asked me for?"

Tessa floundered for words. She couldn't believe how overworked poor Kit was, stranded and trying to handle everything by herself. Yet she'd been so nice to her when she came in anyway. Tessa shot a glance into the restaurant, crammed with customers. "Uh, actually I *do* need a favor. But only on one condition."

"Sure, shoot," replied Kit, sweeping back the red locks that had fallen into her eyes.

"If you'd take *my* credit card for the room instead of Dillon's money and do a little something extra for me, I promise I'll help you in the restaurant tonight till you close. Okay?"

"Oh my gosh!" Kit leaned over the desk and threw her thin arms around Tessa before she knew what hit her. "That would be a godsend! I'll give you half my paycheck and tips, honest—"

"No way," Tessa shook her head. "I'm in Bandits Hollow to stay, no matter what those Iron Feather brothers say. And it won't hurt to make a new friend or two, right? All I ask is that you take this cash," she grabbed the bills, "and put it in an envelope addressed to Dillon Iron Feather. Then mail it first thing tomorrow morning."

"That's it? My pleasure!" Kit enthused, her face visibly relieved.

"Before you mail it," Tessa instructed with a wicked glint in her eye, "I want you to write a simple note and slip it inside."

Kit opened a drawer in the reception desk and pulled out a pen and a notepad. She glanced expectantly at Tessa.

"Dear Dillon Iron Feather," Tessa enunciated, giving Kit a slight smirk. "Go to hell."

6

"Yeehaw-yeehaw," chimed the buckaroo clock on the wall as it struck seven AM in the Golden Wagon Restaurant the following morning. Tessa yawned, watching the cowboy on the bronco rock back and forth on the clock, waving his hat. Despite working her rear end off last night at the banquet to help Kit, she'd decided to slip into the cowhide booth early that morning and grab a bite to eat before plotting how to return to her mine. Hopefully, without getting shot by Dillon Iron Feather.

"Coffee?" asked a woman with a *Lila* name tag. Her hourglass figure filled the peach Victorian dress to nearly bursting, her smile beaming sunshine. "You look like you could use a picker upper, honey."

"Sure," replied Tessa, brooding over her next moves. She cleared her throat. "You don't happen to have loose tea leaves or something that might help foresee my future, do you?"

"Heck, if that were the case," Lila laughed, "we'd have

customers lining out the door!" She poured coffee into a mug and set a small pitcher of cream on the table. Studying Tessa for a moment, she perched her hand on her hip. "Tell me straight. Did you wrong him, or did he wrong you? That look on your face certainly tells a story. And I've lived long enough to know that's what most problems come down to."

"Hmm, maybe both, I guess." Tessa rubbed her brows in fatigue. "Truth be told, I tangled with Dillon Iron Feather yesterday."

"And lived to tell the tale? That's more than can be said for most folks." Lila grinned. "By the way, thanks a million for covering the banquet last night. I had a nasty bug that made me weak with a temperature and had to hit the hay before nightfall. Luckily, I'm all better today."

"No problem." Tessa lifted her mug with a smile. "Good thing that green Victorian dress they had in the back fit me okay. By the way, do ranchers around here always try to pinch new waitresses in town?"

"You betcha." Lila leaned toward Tessa and lowered her voice. "Did Kit show you the trick for keeping them from getting too fresh?"

"You mean kicking them in the shins? It kind of backfired—they liked me *better* afterwards." Tessa sighed. "They said with my sass, I'd make a good ranch wife. Every time I let one of those guys have it, he tipped me twice as much."

"Welcome to Bandits Hollow!" Lila's eyes twinkled. "Watch out, you might get lassoed by one of them. You ready to order, hon?" She glanced left and right. "I'm gonna get you the sirloin breakfast platter," she whispered. "It's free once a week for staff. Nell loves to spoil us—and you sure worked your fair share last night. Kit said you refused to take a dime."

Before Tessa could respond, Lila had already written down the order and was making a beeline for the kitchen to give it to the cook.

"Boy, are you in trouble, missy!" bellowed a woman with gray hair who burst into the restaurant. She wore a smartly-tailored blue rodeo shirt embroidered with yellow roses and a matching skirt and cowboy boots. Wagging a finger at Tessa, she headed straight for her booth and plopped down across from her.

Tessa gazed at her wide eyed, wringing her hands beneath the table. From the looks of her, she figured the woman was Nell, the owner of the hotel and restaurant, who Kit said was in her late sixties. Tessa worried that maybe one of the ranchers last night wasn't too happy with the bruise he'd gotten on his shin after all, and had called Nell to complain. The last thing she wanted was for poor Kit to get in trouble for enlisting help.

"I'll have you know," the woman perched her elbows on the table and glared, "that my employee Kit spilled the beans on you. Who said you were allowed to work here without pay?"

"Um, she was desperate," Tessa replied. "Everyone else was sick, and I couldn't leave her alone in the lurch—"

The woman reached out to grasp Tessa's hand, her gaze changing from cross to the epitome of warmth. She gave her fingers a squeeze. "Well, I'm Nell Granger, and I want to thank you personally," she said in a sincere tone. "Without you, I don't think Kit would have survived that Cattlemen

Association's banquet. It turned out to be our biggest money maker of the year. I certainly am indebted to you, Miss…"

"Grove," she smiled. "Tessa Grove."

"Well, you've got a job here with your name on it if you ever need one. Kit said she made more tips last night than ever before."

Tessa twisted in her seat a little. "I really appreciate your offer," she replied. "But I, uh, have a job actually. I'm a jewelry designer."

"In Bandits Hollow?" Nell raised a brow. "I wasn't aware of a new store opening in town—"

"What I mean is, I inherited my grandfather's mine not too far from here. I intend to work it and make my own creations."

"Good for you!" Nell's face crinkled into a smile. "I always love it when people take a chance in life. And there's no better place than Bandits Hollow. That's why I bought the hotel and restaurant here a decade ago."

"Really?" Tessa's face brightened with hope.

"Sure! My husband and I were in Nebraska, our kids all grown, and we decided to go for it. So we uprooted to run this business in the most beautiful place on earth. It was a hell of a fixer upper back then, and we worked our tails off to make it what you see today. But a year after we opened our doors, Harold passed on."

"Oh, I'm so sorry," Tessa said in a soft voice. "I know what it's like to be…alone."

Nell nodded. "So, you heading out to your mine this morning?"

"Well, it's not quite that easy." Drawing a deep breath,

Tessa pulled out her grandfather's mining claim and map and showed it to Nell, feeling a strange kinship with her. After all, Nell had taken a gamble in life, too. Maybe things didn't turn out the way she wanted, but she'd made it work, right? Tessa studied the map, feeling compelled to spill the truth. "The problem is that my mine is on Dillon Iron Feather's ranch."

"Ranch? You mean those old ramshackle buildings he cleaned out a few months ago? Because the BLM believed him when he showed them an old boulder marked with symbols proving his ancestor had gotten the place from the Utes? Honey, no one's ever technically ranched there. That place was a hideout for the Bandits Hollow Gang—the namesake of our town."

Tessa's eyes grew the size of the restaurant's pancakes. Her mind reeled over the thought of outlaw spirits still lingering over Dillon's place. "S-So what draws him there now?" She took an apprehensive sip of coffee.

"Well, if you follow sports much," Nell sighed, "you'd know he decided to ditch his fighting career after winning his last match."

"I heard the rumors," Tessa admitted.

"Rumors ain't the same as fact, sweetheart. I've known those Iron Feather boys ever since they were teens and got sent to that godforsaken reform school. Sure, they were troubled and got into lots of scrapes with the law after their folks died. The courts deemed them a criminal menace and wouldn't even let me take them in. But there's an honor in the Iron Feather brothers born of hard times and looking out for one another." Nell narrowed her gaze. "Dillon didn't kill that man in the fight. He put him in a coma. And six months later, the fella woke up and is now recovering. It's anybody's guess if he'll ever walk again, but he sure as hell won't fight. One thing's for certain, though—Dillon left a very lucrative career because his conscience wouldn't let him go into the ring anymore."

Tessa shook her head, puzzled. "Why not? I mean, if he won the fight and was making money and everything?"

Nell studied a red-bandana napkin on the table for a moment, her eyes following the small flowers and paisley swirls on the cloth. She lifted her gaze to Tessa as if measuring her depth of character. "Dillon knew the next guy he fought would be dead," she said in a grave tone. "He didn't want to do that to somebody—to their family. He knows what it's like to lose your parents."

Tessa stared into her mug with a lump in her throat, recalling the pain from the loss of her own mother as if it were yesterday. She couldn't say she'd entirely recovered. Maybe no one ever does. Yet one more reason to make my dream a reality, she thought. *Life is short, and it's what my mother would have wanted for me.*

"I ain't saying Dillon's a saint," Nell added. She held up her coffee mug for Lila to come by. "None of those Iron Feather brothers are. All of them are angry and mean as sin. They just deal with it in different ways."

When Lila refilled her coffee, Nell took a few sips. "Dillon fights like a hired killer. Barrett pushes the law to a point that's probably pathological. And their youngest brother Lander is obsessed with being the biggest rancher in the county, beating all the other guys. None of it works, of course—they don't have a lick of peace inside."

"I guess I don't understand." Tessa's brows furrowed. "What's filled them with so much hostility?"

Nell fell silent for a moment and tilted her head back, gazing at the elk antler light fixture above her. Her lips pursed a little as she became lost in thought. "I expect it has something to do with their ancestor Iron Feather. He was part Apache, part Ute, and part God knows what. But the fact that he was considered a breed and a famous outlaw, with magical powers to boot—that's enough to make kids tease you awful hard when you go to school. To this day, folks still love to trade nasty gossip about them and give them a wide berth. It doesn't help that Dillon looks just like Iron Feather."

Nell pointed to sepia-toned photo in a wood frame decorated with barbed wire on a wall nearby. Among a group of white men in nineteenth-century garb was a tall Native American man in a long black coat and deerskin pants who was the spitting image of Dillon. He wore a black, flat-brimmed hat with an owl feather tucked into the band. Tessa blinked, astounded at the resemblance.

"That photo is of the Bandits Hollow Gang. I suppose if folks brand you an outlaw when you're young for long enough, you'll up and act like one." Nell drained her coffee. "But that don't mean Dillon ain't got a heart. All them Iron Feather boys try to hide it best they can, but sometimes it leaks out. Like the fact that Dillon paid all of his opponent's hospital bills while he was in a coma."

Tessa gasped—bills like that must have soared into thousands of dollars. She was shocked to hear such a thing about a man who seemed stern and downright...lethal. "He did try to pay for my room," she conceded. "But I make it a policy never to depend on favors from men."

"Atta girl," Nell chimed in approval. Her gaze slid to Lila ushering a group of ranchers to a table by the large, river rock fireplace. They were all wearing Stetson hats and cowboy boots with spurs that jangled against the floor boards while they walked. Lila chided them about taking off their hats indoors.

"I want you to promise me one thing." Nell held up a finger to Lila to indicate she was ordering the number one on the menu—pancakes and homemade sausage. "Don't you dare let none of those Iron Feather boys bully you away from what you know is yours. All right?" She picked up the mining claim map and studied it carefully. "Dillon hasn't had that ranch for very long, and this road you share," she tapped the page, "looks like it was built by *your* ancestor, not his. So since you wouldn't take any pay, I'm going to loan you something for helping me out last night."

To Tessa's astonishment, Nell reached into her skirt pocket and pulled out a small pistol with her name engraved on the handle. She laid it on the table.

"Mining's tough, honey. There ain't a prospector in the county that doesn't carry a weapon to defend his claim. And enemies can pop out of the woodwork that you never saw coming. If Dillon or anybody else gives you trouble about being at that mine the law says you have a right to, you just show them this and act like you mean business. They'll skedaddle soon enough."

Nell nodded at the group of ranchers by the fireplace, some of whom Tessa recognized from the banquet last night.

"When my Harold died, a few of those ol' boys got the notion that they'd push me and my hotel business around. Big mistake." She scanned Tessa up and down as if weighing her grit. "You gotta be strong to make it here in Bandits Hollow," she warned. "And that means you don't back down for nothin'."

Nell pulled a lock of hair from the coiled bun on her head that was held together by a silver concho barrette. She lifted up the thick gray strands laced with streaks of blonde. "When folks see a tow-headed woman like I was in those days working hard on her dream, well, they tend to assume she can be run over."

She pushed the pistol toward Tessa. "It's up to women like you and me to prove them wrong." Nell leaned back in the booth and folded her arms, giving Tessa a knowing smile.

"Dead wrong."

7

Tessa gazed at the dusky morning sky with a hint of blue over the mountains, traces of snow dotting the jagged peaks. She huddled her down jacket tighter and sucked up her courage, marching with determined strides to the old mine door. It was only eight AM, and Nell had dropped her off at the start of Grove Road so she could walk silently on the dirt to the mine and not disturb Dillon.

"You call me lickety-split if you need anything, okay?" Nell had said before she drove off. "Trust me on this one—you don't want to give Dillon a reason to train his shotgun on you if he hears you coming, so keep quiet. If he gets in your way, tell him he'll have to answer to *me*."

Nell's support lent Tessa the nerve she needed to press forward, and fortunately Dusty had dropped off her luggage at the hotel the night before. Now she had her clothes and jewelry tools, some supplies she'd gotten from the General

Mercantile, plus a backpack Nell had loaned her filled with a pick and a small shovel.

And Nell's pistol.

Along with a silencer Nell had retrieved from an old safe inside the hotel.

When Tessa reached the mine, she set her luggage and backpack down on the frosty ground and pulled out the gun. Her heart began to wobble. Sure, she knew she had a legal right to open this mine, even if it meant shooting off the rusty lock her grandfather had left on the door. But handling guns made her squeamish. She glanced around the ranch, making sure no one was watching, then bit her lip and fired the weapon.

The old padlock burst into pieces. Despite her trembling hand, the pines nearby resumed with the early morning sounds of birds. Relieved to have succeeded, Tessa pushed hard against the mine door, but it wouldn't budge. She kicked it a few times to no avail. Finally, at the count of three, she threw her shoulder against the door with all her might, wedging it open a little. With several more shoves, she managed to open the heavy mine door, and she peered into the darkness shrouded by long, draping cobwebs. Something flew past her, rifling her hair, and it made her jump.

Bats.

Three of them bolted from the mine and flitted into the woods.

Tessa's skittering pulse was hardly soothed by the sight, but she bent to the ground anyway and pulled out a flashlight from her backpack. Drawing a deep breath, she worked up the mettle to step into the unknown depths of the mine. It was about a foot taller than her, barely big enough to accommodate a large man, and several feet wide with a fairly smooth dirt floor. Tessa traced the beam of her flashlight along the dusty rock wall. Spitting into her palm, she rubbed her hand against the grimy stones. Along with granite, smoky quartz and fluorite were revealed, minerals that were typical for gold country. But she doubted there were any veins of gold left, or this mine would have been carved out with bigger dimensions by now. Still, she was aware New Age enthusiasts loved smoky quartz for its mystical powers and fluorite for the psychic protection it was supposed to offer, and she'd made many designs with those stones for customers of Jacquier & Co. At least the minerals she'd found on the wall would give her a good start for making her own jewelry. Curious, she shot her flashlight beam farther into the mine, its light eventually fading into the darkness. I'll go deeper and explore later on, she thought, when I can get a lantern to help me see better.

"Need a little more light?" a man's voice called out.

Tessa whipped around, only to see the bright corona of a mega-watt flashlight meeting her gaze. Nearly blinded, her body stiffened. She was glad she'd slipped that pistol into her jacket pocket.

"Who are you?" she demanded, cradling her fingers around the handle of Nell's gun, just in case.

"A neighbor," the man replied casually. "But I could be a good friend, depending on how you look at it."

He lowered his flashlight to the ground, and in the daylight that filtered through the mine entrance, she began to make out the features of a middle-aged man in a western plaid shirt and jeans, with the well-worn hat and cowboy boots typical of local ranchers. In fact, she recognized him from the Golden Wagon Restaurant, when she'd been talking to Nell. He'd sat across from them with the group of ranchers that Nell confessed had once given her trouble. Tessa's breath hitched when she realized he must have overheard their conversation about her mine and decided to follow her here this morning.

What a creep—

"Doesn't look like this old cave has much to offer," the man remarked. He cast his flashlight beam on the rock walls. "If it ever did. I'm Bill Crouch, by the way. My ranch backs up to Grove Road."

He moved forward to shake Tessa's hand. She responded by taking a step back and stubbornly keeping her distance.

"I'm surprised you haven't gotten shot already," she noted. "Since you must have crossed Dillon Iron Feather's land to get here."

"Well, I parked down the road and walked like you did, to avoid that embarrassment." He gave her an easy smile. "Everybody knows not to disturb Dillon—"

"What do you want?" Tessa interrupted. "It must be pretty important to have you getting up at the crack of dawn to stalk me."

"Oh, I wouldn't call it stalking," Bill laughed. "More like tracking you down to make a decent offer. Here," he pulled out a roll of bills, "this is five thousand dollars for the rights to this mine. In cash—no strings attached." He held out the money to her. "That ought to get you started in your jewelry business, or whatever it is you came to Colorado for."

Heat bristled against Tessa's cheeks. So Bill *had* eavesdropped about that part of her life when she'd talked to Nell. All at once, his uninvited company made her feel alone and vulnerable. She searched the ground, trying to think of a way to get rid of him without blasting a hole through his chest, when a long shadow seeped across the floor of the mine, reaching to her feet.

"Shouldn't a deal like that be made in the light of day, instead of this dark hole?"

Tessa turned to see a tall silhouette at the entrance of the mine. It filled the entire doorway.

Dillon Iron Feather.

"You ain't got no business here." Bill spun to face him. "This ain't your mine."

"He's right, it's not," Tessa echoed. "But that won't influence my decision much, because my answer is no."

Strangely enough, Tessa felt comforted by Dillon's presence. He may be hostile and trigger happy as hell, she thought, but at least he didn't stalk me out of the blue like Bill Crouch.

"Why on earth are you so eager to get this mine?" she asked Bill. "Especially after you claimed it's tapped out?"

"He doesn't give a rip about the mine," Dillon said, walking up to the two of them. "He wants what it's next to."

Dillon pointed to the nearby mountain they could see from the entrance of the mine. "Rumor has it a new gold vein's been discovered a mile in that direction. If Bill tunnels toward it, even illegally, he might be able to tap into it. And no one will ever know—"

"Fifty-thousand," Bill cut in. "Lady, that's the offer of the century. This mine ain't held nothin' for a hundred years. You'd be a fool not to take it."

Holy cow! Tessa thought, her heart throbbing against her chest to the point of pain. She'd never seen that kind of money before, and it could be a whopping seed investment for her jewelry business. But she knew if she accepted it, she'd spend the rest of her life scrambling for quality stones on the open market, competing with the likes of Arthur Jacquier for each one. This mine—and the minerals inside it—would always be *hers*. She was in competition with no one, calling her own shots.

At that moment, an owl hooted nearby, making Tessa nearly leap out of her skin. Its deep call reverberated off the walls of the mine and penetrated into the darkness. For reasons she couldn't explain, she felt as if the echo vibrated through her heart as well. When the sound stopped, the air around her felt thicker, full of presence, like something mysterious had entered their space and caused the molecules to shift. Tessa gazed at Bill Crouch in the swath of her flashlight. Though his round, neighborly face was etched with deep wrinkles from his broad smile, his blue eyes appeared strangely cold—

Just like Arthur Jacquier, she thought. Whenever he tried to own my soul.

Tessa shook her head, but she couldn't shed Bill's gaze from her mind. Shoring up her resolve, she brushed past both men and marched to the entrance of the mine. When she reached the meadow, thin rays of sunlight broke over her face, warming her skin a little. She turned to face the men, who were heading to join her. She knew it might seem like the stupidest decision of her whole life, but inside, she refused to hop from one cage in New York to another in Colorado. And Bill Crouch's big fat wallet would close off this mine to her for good.

Along with her dreams.

"Sixty-thousand," Bill persisted, walking straight up to Tessa and leaning into her face. His doughy features were creased with the kind of smile that made her sick. "Think of the possibilities."

To Tessa's surprise, Dillon wedged between her and Bill, his whole body in a protective stance. Though he didn't have a shotgun this time, the way he folded his arms with his muscles stretched tight against his denim shirt made it clear he was every bit as deadly.

"She already gave you her answer, Crouch. Your forefathers were never able to wrangle this land from the Utes, no matter how many lawsuits your people hit them with. And you're not getting access to it now."

"She didn't respond to my final offer," Bill reminded him, peering over Dillon's shoulder at Tessa. "Let her speak for herself. You're not the only one here who can talk, Mister Mixed Breed."

Bill's eyes glinted with smug, good ol' boy mirth. But Tessa hadn't forgotten for a second the chilling look she'd seen on him earlier.

"You and your money—get off this land," she demanded.

She stepped around Dillon and faced Bill head on, reaching into her pocket and holding up Nell's pistol. Her palms clutched the handle where Nell's name was inscribed, hoping to channel her strength. Slowly, she slid her finger to linger over the trigger.

"Move it—right now. Unless you feel like being buried here."

8

Dillon and Tessa watched dust clouds swallow Bill's form as he walked as fast as he could muster down the road, disappearing from view.

"I like your style." A smile teased at Dillon's lips. "You would've shot him, wouldn't you? If he didn't leave."

Tessa was still trying to regulate her breaths and calm down, feeling nearly ready to throw up. She couldn't believe she'd actually threatened a man's life! Who had she become since she'd left New York? Sure, she'd seen her share of rough situations as a cab driver, but nothing face-to-face quite like this—

"H-How do you know?" she sputtered.

Dillon fell quiet. He dug at a patch of soil with his boot, lifting a few old leaves and turning them over to examine their damp edges, which had been hidden against the earth. He glanced up and looked her in the eye.

"Because you've got no place else to go."

Damn, he nailed it, Tessa thought. Though she admired Dillon's powers of observation, she prayed the embarrassment didn't show too much on her cheeks.

"I know an orphan when I see one," he stated. "When you first got here, I figured you were the daughter of some New York stockbroker or socialite with big ideas about investing in gold."

"And now?" She held her breath, a bit afraid of what he might say.

Dillon studied her face, his deep brown eyes searching hers until he appeared satisfied he'd sorted out the layers of some mystery. His silence became interminable, and it made her uneasy.

"You don't have a damn thing but this mine, do you? And you're going to hang on to it with all you've got," he finally surmised. "The world has not been kind to you, Miss Grove. It's written all over your face. But you're living on hope anyway."

Tessa felt as though he'd torn her heart from her chest and ripped it open for the world to see. How could he read me so perfectly like that? she thought, clenching her fists. Tears of frustration blurred the edges of her vision. She folded her arms and tried to will them to stop.

"Y-You don't even know me!" she protested. "I don't see how you can possibly presume—"

Dillon held up his hand.

"It takes one to know one. A wolf on its own in the wilderness can't fool another lone wolf."

With that, Dillon edged closer. All at once, his hard, muscular body and the scent of pine smoke and saddle leather that clung to his skin were more than ruggedly sexy. He felt near, way too near, as though he'd slipped into a chamber of her soul without her realizing it. Tessa trembled, but for the life of her, she couldn't break away.

"The hunger in your eyes betrays everything," he whispered.

Breathless, she struggled for air as if the wind had been knocked out of her. Damn him all to hell! Tessa thought. She swallowed hard, trying to fake her composure. But at this point she knew she was out of arguments, which Dillon obviously could see through anyway. Gazing at the entrance of the mine, at the large dark mouth that might devour her dreams if she wasn't careful, she cleared her throat.

"Dillon," she dared to broach the subject that could ignite a firestorm between them, "I know you don't want me here. And we both know I'm not about to leave. So for the sake of, well, conjecture I guess, I was just wondering…"

"Say it," Dillon admonished impatiently.

Tessa stared at the ground. "Do you, you know," she began, feeling her heart climb into her throat, "think the idea of pulling something valuable out of this old mine is…crazy?"

When she glanced up at his face, she could have sworn he stood taller. Dillon's square jaw was set with a hard-earned pride. His intense, dark eyes locked on hers, making her deeply uncomfortable.

"If there's anything at all worthwhile in that mine," his voice was so low and certain it made her shiver, "you've shown me this morning you've got the guts to pull it out. But the problem is," Dillon crossed his arms, as intimidating as ever, "you're on *my* land."

"Technically, this section *isn't* your land," she corrected. "Do I have to show you my map and claim again?" Tessa thrust up her chin, refusing to be dismissed so easily. Heart racing, she willed her body to stretch to her full height and thrust her hand into her pocket. "Or how about my pistol—"

Dillon's lips curled when she yanked the weapon from her jacket, albeit with a shaky grip.

"Well who am I to argue with an armed woman?" He lifted his hands with a killer smile that nearly knocked her off her feet. Then his twinkling eyes became darker. "But this is the last time you'll ever see me without a weapon, Miss Grove. Even at dawn."

He turned away and began to walk toward the deep recesses of the mine, motioning for her to follow.

"Come on, city girl," Dillon said. "It's time to take a look at what you've got."

"Hand me the feather, please," Tessa insisted in a flinty tone. "My grandfather willed it to *me*, you know."

She watched Dillon flinch, clearly irked by her legal entitlement to his ancestor's medicine. He rolled up the denim sleeves of his shirt and struck a match to light two lanterns on the ground. After they'd walked far enough into the mine that not even her flashlight was of much use, he'd left for a few minutes to grab the lanterns from the barn and brought them back. Now he held one up at eye level, staring at its hissing kerosene flame.

"This owl feather came from a revered Native American

man." Dillon slowly removed the feather from his back pocket. "I've never seen it before you arrived, only heard about it from legend. I have no idea what it can do, Miss Grove—and neither do you. Do you understand what I'm saying?"

He held the feather out to her like an offering.

She nodded, uncertain now about the responsibility of taking it.

"I will provide one suggestion though," he said.

Tessa opened her palms, waiting for his advice. He set the feather lightly across her hands. It felt as soft as falling snow.

"Make sure you know what you really want when you hold this feather. I mean that."

Tingles chased through Tessa's arms, just like they had when she first plucked the feather from her grandfather's cigar box in New York. She swiftly tucked it into her belt. Picking up the other lantern, she hoisted her backpack onto her shoulders, leaving her other luggage at the entrance of the mine. "You ready?" she said, trying to hide the apprehension in her voice. She straightened her back. "Let's scope out what the mine has to offer."

When she stepped forward with her lantern raised, illuminating a much wider radius of warm light, the mine began to appear entirely different. The hues of the walls were golden now, with traces of occasional color visible in the surrounding ore.

"I guess you know from my conversation with Bill Crouch that I'm a jeweler," she mentioned to Dillon. "I don't truck in diamonds, if that's what you're thinking. Only American gems and metals. That's why this mine is important to me, even if all I can find are semi-precious stones."

She tilted her lantern and pointed to a thin vein of purple and blue on the wall with hints of green. Reaching out her arm to rub it hard with her sleeve, she made the colors more visible. "This fluorite is fairly common in states with gold like Colorado. And it's pretty when it's all shined up. But as a gem, it's hardness is only about four on the Mohs scale." Tessa plucked a dusty white rock from the ground. "That means I can easily scratch it with something that's a six in hardness, like this piece of quartz."

She carved the rock into the fluorite and swung her lantern closer, revealing a light scar. "If fluorite or smoky quartz are all I can find here," she continued, "I'll still make them shine with my silver designs. Then I'll be able to sell them to retailers with…um…integrity."

"Integrity," Dillon nodded. "That's important to you."

Something about the way he said it made Tessa choke up a little. She glanced aside to hide her reaction. "Well, when you've worked for years driving a taxi on a meter," she sighed, "or felt like merely a number creating someone else's jewelry, it's kind of," she searched for the right words, "refreshing, I suppose…"

"To finally be yourself?"

Dillon had swiped the words straight from her heart. The lightning-fast way he finished her sentence made it seem like he understood. Like maybe he knew how it felt to slowly betray yourself and want to change course. For the first time, in the soft lantern light, she noticed there was a lattice of scars all over Dillon's hands, permanent reminders of his years as a fighter. What on earth made him want to be a rancher, she wondered, when he could have pursued anything after his

MMA career? And why did he decide to go with me into this mine anyway, when at first he wanted to run me off his land?

She shot a glance at Dillon, spying a hint of tenderness in his brown eyes. All at once, he no longer appeared as formidable as before. If she didn't know better, she'd say the look on his face seemed downright…encouraging, like he was urging her on.

Oh my God, Tessa realized, he's rooting for the underdog, isn't he? She held her breath, a bit stunned. It was then she noticed the deep scars on his jaw, too. Slowly, it dawned on her that he'd been the underdog during his reform school days, like Nell had said. And though his hard, towering physique was nothing to mess with now, he probably never forgot what that felt like.

Dillon was close enough that Tessa caught more nuances from the scent of his skin revealing a warm fragrance, like sunshine on old barn wood. And there were faint traces of spices, like sage or perhaps chipotle pepper. She couldn't help thinking that his iron body, with his powerful arms and strapping chest, were so inviting to the touch. The second that notion whisked through her brain, she yanked back her lantern and hugged it close, surprised at herself.

An inkling of a smile traced over Dillon's lips.

She caught the way his eyes lingered over her cheek and heart-shaped chin, falling to the curves of her breasts and hips, apparent even in her puffy down jacket and jeans. His gaze returned to the vibrance of her eyes.

Dillon wriggled something from his jeans pocket. "I had a feeling this might come in handy."

He held up a small piece of turquoise, its deep blue color

tinged with green. For a moment, he looked like he was comparing it to the rich blue-green of her eyes.

Tessa had seen a lot of turquoise come her way at Jacquier & Co., but none that compared to this. Turquoise had been a favorite among Arthur's clientele since it came from the American Southwest. But most of the varieties she'd worked with had a black, spider-web matrix against a vivid blue, or were infused with golden brown tones highlighting aqua green. This piece had deep blue and green tones set off by lacy wisps of gold in the matrix, making it the most stunning piece of turquoise she'd ever seen.

"Where on earth did you get this?" she asked.

"You're not the only one who received an inheritance from Iron Feather."

Tessa spotted a sparkle in Dillon's eye.

"Go ahead—touch it," he invited.

She reached out her finger, prepared to snap it back if something strangely magical happened. After all, this belonged to Iron Feather.

"It's—it's warm," she observed. "Warmer than it could be from your pocket. Like it's…emitting heat. How's that possible?"

Dillon shrugged. "I only know bits and pieces of the wisdom Iron Feather shared. Things my parents told me before they passed on. History books don't record that kind of knowledge." He gazed at the chunk of turquoise, and his eyes caught hers. "But I think the heat means you're not wasting your time here."

He set down his lantern and slipped the backpack from her shoulders. Unzipping it, he pulled out several tools.

"You wanted a mine, Miss Grove." He handed her a pick and a shovel, while he grabbed a large mallet. Side-stepping a few yards from her, he swung the mallet at the rock with every ounce of force in his being. Rock fragments exploded from the wall and crumbled to the ground as his impact echoed through the mine like a blast of dynamite. When the sound faded, Dillon turned to Tessa with a smile.

"Time to start digging, city girl."

9

"Stop!" Tessa sank her fingers into Dillon's arm, using all her weight to pull him back from the wall and prohibit his next strike. She stared at the ground, speechless.

"What? What is it?" Dillon set down his mallet, searching the dirt for what held her interest.

She stooped to pick up several hunks of rock that had been loosened by Dillon's blows. Standing up to gaze at the wall, she scrutinized the uneven surface. Swiftly, she grabbed her backpack and fished around, pulling out a small black box that had a lens attached at the top.

"Here," she handed Dillon her lantern.

While he watched, she grasped a vial of rubbing alcohol and a rag from her backpack and cleaned one of the stray stones. Then she opened the lid of the black box and applied a drop of oil from another vial to the center and set the stone in the middle, closing the lid and flipping on a switch. A light beamed from within.

Tessa peered through the lens. "C-Can it be?" she muttered. She pulled back and blinked several times. Rubbing her eyes, she looked again. "It *is* arid here, with high altitude. And there are fractures from crustal uplifts everywhere."

She gazed at a blue vein that Dillon's mallet had exposed on the wall and looked one more time into her scope. "Copper, aluminum, iron. They've all been mined in the Rocky Mountains, not to mention gold. It's the perfect host rock—"

"Probably amazonite," Dillon offered, studying the vein. "It's very blue, and there's an abandoned mine of that stuff on a ranch about half an hour from here. A few years ago it fetched a decent price, according to one of my neighbors, but the market fell flat."

Tessa shook her head. "I worked with amazonite several times on my last job. This is a refractometer—it measures how light bends when it hits a stone." She stood to her feet and held up the contraption to Dillon. "Amazonite has a refraction index of 1.5. We had to double check all the stones we set where I used to work to make sure there weren't any fakes." She rolled her eyes. "My old boss was pretty paranoid, so I got good at it."

Tessa tilted the refractometer and pointed to a cheat sheet she'd pasted on the bottom with a listing of gems and their indexes. "This stone here," she pulled the chunk of blue rock out from inside the box, "is 1.63."

Her eyes appeared large—in awe, even. Faster than Dillon could ask what the number meant, she set down the meter and grabbed a hunk of quartz from the ground. With all her might, she dove the rock into the blue vein like she was driving a stake into the wall. It didn't make a scratch.

"My God, Dillon!" she gasped. "Quartz is a six on the Mohs hardness scale. This blue vein is *much* harder, like a seven and a half. Nothing in the Southwest is that quality anymore—the best stuff was tapped out decades ago. Jewelers pay a pretty price when they find those older stones on the market. Do you have any idea what this means?"

Dillon dug into his pocket and held out his turquoise piece to her—it perfectly matched the blue vein on the wall. His eyes focused on the dark recesses of the mine as though he'd spied a ghost.

"It means you've found a rare vein of turquoise."

He paused, peering into the darkness with one of his long, infernal silences that drove Tessa crazy. She couldn't help wondering what he was thinking. Yet something inside her knew that wasn't the crux of it at all. With that far-away look in his eyes, it was more like Dillon was *feeling*. Taking the time to register the nuances of some kind of energy she didn't understand. Finally, he turned to her.

"My ancestor Iron Feather is here," he said. "He's watching you."

Thoroughly spooked, Tessa hugged her waist for comfort. She darted a glance to the turquoise in his hand.

"Th-That turquoise he left you," she stammered, "it...it..."

"Must have come from here," Dillon nodded. "Where the Bandits Hollow Gang had their hideout."

At that moment, an owl hooted from outside the mine,

startling Tessa. She figured it was the same owl as before, but that didn't do much to ease her nerves. Dillon's eyes met hers.

"You're supposed to be here," he said softly.

"To make jewelry?" She was puzzled why any ancestral spirit, let alone the essence of some famous outlaw, might give a rip about her chosen profession.

Dillon shook his head. "No, to keep people like Bill Crouch from destroying these stones with his greed for gold. Turquoise is sacred to the Apaches and Utes—the Colorado tribes Iron Feather came from. They call it *dáatł'iiji* or *sakwakar*."

He closed his fingers over the turquoise in his palm and slipped it back into his pocket. Gazing at Tessa, she could have sworn she detected a trace of sensitivity in his eyes, a kind of rare openness, and it surprised her. The second she took notice, Dillon squared his broad shoulders and his face fell to granite once again, totally unreadable.

"I have to go work now."

With no further explanation, Dillon abruptly turned and walked away toward the entrance of the mine.

Tessa sighed, unable to keep from admiring the view of his perfectly-formed backside as he strode off. *Nice ass,* she admitted begrudgingly to herself, biting her lip. *Even if he did hog-tie me once.* Craning her neck, her gaze followed the sway of his long legs until he reached the opening of the mine and disappeared from view.

Glancing down, she scanned the extraordinary stones beside her feet. Prickles of excitement leaped up her spine, making her feel like she'd won the lottery. She picked up a chunk, studying its intense hues of blue and green, when she realized that without *her*, this secret vein of turquoise, once known by Iron Feather, would never have been rediscovered. And she'd protected it from the likes Bill Crouch with a pistol, no less! A bit awed by the brassy woman she'd become since she'd arrived in Colorado, she smirked a little. For now at least, she felt pretty confident that Dillon Iron Feather wasn't going to try and run her off any time soon.

Tessa sat cross-legged on the frosty grass outside the mine with her down jacket hood pulled over her head, trying to stay warm. Though she attempted to busy herself with the new tent she'd purchased at the General Mercantile the day before, a part of her knew the goosebumps on her skin weren't just because of the cold. No matter how thrilled she was to discover high-grade turquoise inside her very own claim, Dillon's mysterious words about his ancestor kept spooling through her mind, leaving her rattled. Was her mine—and the stones it contained—haunted?

She turned her head, watching Dillon over by the barn. He was saddling up a large chestnut horse with a pack mule tethered to it. When he finished cinching the girth, he mounted the horse and went up a trail that appeared to head for the mountains with the mule in tow. Tessa had no idea what business occupied him that required a pack mule at nine in the morning. But whatever it was, his face appeared determined, and he apparently needed an enormous bow and a quiver of arrows that he'd tied to the mule's back.

Opening a giant plastic bag beside her suitcase, she pulled out the tent and a sleeping bag that she'd also bought at the General Mercantile. She set her sights on the mine entrance, where she intended to leave her tent until it got dark. Then she'd bring it outside to the meadow as soon as she saw Dillon retire to his cabin for the evening—because there was no way she was going to sleep inside that eerie cave all night long. At dawn, she'd quickly take the tent apart and hide it again in the mine.

The only problem was, she'd never assembled a tent before.

Okay, so I'm from Brooklyn, and my mom didn't happen to take me camping every summer, she thought, bracing herself for the task. And I never exactly informed Dillon that I'm staying right here till I'm done with my mining. But somebody has to fend off the Bill Crouches of the world, right? I'm pretty sure Dillon's brother Barrett will back me up if any of the ranch neighbors come stalking again.

Gathering her nerve, Tessa untied the strings on the tent and spread out the thin nylon fabric. The tent was flimsy, she had to admit, but at least she was able to connect the poles to create a small dome. Not big enough to stand in by a long shot, but it had enough room for her luggage and supplies, along with four dozen granola bars she'd purchased in Bandits Hollow to keep her going.

Scanning Dillon's property, she eyed an old, vertical wood structure that appeared to be an outhouse. As long as she reminded herself to get more toilet paper and plenty of food and bottled water from town, she figured she was set. All she needed now was to buy a portable, gas generator to power her soldering and polishing tools so she could create a nice pendant to thank Nell for her kindness, and she'd be in business.

Business—

The very word gave Tessa a thrill.

She'd finally become her own woman, ready to create whatever her imagination could conjure and take on all the risks herself. Her jewelry would be the expression of her spirit and the passionate cornerstone of her life.

Tessa smiled—she couldn't possibly be happier.

A warm feeling arose in her chest, and for a moment she leaned down to hug her backpack.

"Thank you, Grandpa," she whispered, pressing her cheek against the canvas. "For believing in me. And you too, Nell."

The morning sun beat intently on her shoulders, invigorating her muscles. She brushed herself off and toted the small, domed tent into the entrance of the mine. Then she returned to sling the backpack over her shoulder and grab a few more supplies.

"Time to get to work," she muttered, feeling optimistic. She reached inside the front pocket of her backpack and pulled out a chocolate-chip granola bar to celebrate the moment. It was her favorite kind, and she ripped open the wrapper to take a few greedy bites. The extra burst of energy was just what she needed to tackle the tedious hand-mining she knew was ahead of her to pull out the turquoise without damaging it.

When she stuffed the wrapper into her backpack pocket,

she smiled wistfully at the mine, imagining the kinds of boutiques that might one day carry her jewelry. "Come hell or high water," Tessa declared, "I'm going to make a name for myself in this world. No more being a number."

10

Something raked softly against Tessa's cheek in the dark, interrupting her sleep. It felt strangely like the fingers of a...

Ghost.

Holy crap, she thought, barely awake when she rolled away from the nylon wall of her tent. Was I dreaming? Could there be coyotes sniffing around? What if it's the phantom of—

Iron Feather...

She bolted to a sitting position and fumbled with her sleeping bag, feeling like a butterfly trying to shake a cocoon. When she finally managed to wriggle free, fear riddled her body in waves. She dove for her backpack to grab her flashlight and turned it on, hoping to scare away the intruder—spirit or otherwise.

Nevertheless, a large shadow grew against the wall of her tent.

Get the pistol—quick, she told herself. She seized the weapon from her backpack and set down her flashlight. The large shadow could be a trick of the light beam, she reasoned, squinting and attempting to slow her breaths. But what if it's Bill Crouch again, ready to try something more forceful this time? She clasped the pistol in both hands to keep the barrel from shaking.

"Back off!" she commanded. "Or I swear I'll shoot—"

Trying to contain her panic, she crawled to the door and unzipped the fly, peeking out her head. All she could see in the darkness was a massive black figure beside her tent.

It stood up…

As tall as a man.

That's no wayward coyote, she realized.

"I told you I'll shoot!" Tessa threatened again, waving her pistol.

Heart galloping, she struggled for a moment to unscrew the silencer from the gun. Then she fired a warning shot in the air to show she was serious. The blast echoed over the mountains, seeming to rise to the stars.

A peculiar snapping sound issued from the intruder, combined with deep-throated grunts. Within seconds, the black figure overwhelmed the small tent and tackled her to the ground, making her fingers lose their grip on the gun. Heavy blows boxed against her head while her screams filled the night.

"Tessa!" She heard Dillon call out. "God no—Tessa! Play dead!"

Claws broke through her shirt and sliced against her back. Too petrified to move any longer, she took Dillon's advice and allowed her body to go limp. It required every ounce of courage she had to steel herself and not cry out in fear.

Another gunshot split the night.

A huge weight fell against her, crushing her with fur as thick as buffalo hide. For a moment, she couldn't breathe, feeling like she'd been buried alive. All at once, the weight mysteriously rolled off her body. Tessa found herself rising in air, held tight against Dillon's chest. She was being carried in his arms.

"No—no!" he cried. "Hang in there—don't pass out on me!"

She could feel Dillon's heart hammering through his shirt as his legs drummed beneath them. She didn't know how long he'd been running, but soon she heard the creak of a door. Her body slowly descended into the softness of a wide bed.

The wounds on her back ignited with intense pain the second she came into contact with the bedspread, and it made her wail. Yet her voice seemed oddly far away, growing thinner by the second, as if it were being syphoned from her throat. Her eyesight was hazy and soon began to darken at the edges, like she was falling down a well.

Before long, Tessa passed out.

"How could you have camped out there? You don't know a damn thing about the wilderness! You could've been killed—"

She heard Dillon's voice as though it came from the remnants of a dream. Somewhere between sleep and waking, sounds filtered into her ears, stray words that competed with the loud ringing tone in her brain.

Gently, Dillon rolled her body over. Even in her haze, Tessa caught a world of concern in his eyes. His tender gaze traveled over her, wincing at the extent of her wounds. He began to pull off all her clothes.

"This gonna hurt like hell," he warned.

He dabbed a soft fabric onto her skin that burned like a fire, but Tessa was too delirious to react. The air around them smelled of rubbing alcohol, probably from the vial in her backpack. Dillon carefully patted her back and shoulder with a dry cloth and applied a thick, oily substance to her skin, like a salve or poultice. It reeked of juniper, sage, and tree bark mixed with wild animal fat.

Then he wrapped her up in a large, soft hide to cover her naked body. To her surprise, he held her firm in his arms as if he were a human bandage of healing. Slowly, he began to sway back and forth. A low and beautiful chant came from his lips in a language she didn't understand. Dillon hugged her even tighter, the heat of him as warm and close now as though they'd become one person. She didn't have the strength to bristle against his peculiar ritual, so she allowed herself surrender to his embrace while his chants vibrated from his chest through the hide.

As the warmth between them grew, the concoction he'd applied to her wounds no longer burned on her skin. All pain began to disappear, seeming to be absorbed into the hide or whisked away by the unusual tones of his song. Tessa narrowed her eyes for a moment, yet everything remained a blur. Feeling weak, she let her head fall against his broad chest.

At that moment, Dillon fell silent, holding her so close it made her feel like they'd somehow fused with the hide.

"Dammit, I should have checked on you," he berated himself in a low whisper. He caressed her hair and rested his warm hand on her cheek. She could feel his worried pulse beating rapidly through his palm. "You stubborn woman." His arms cinched hard. "I should have known you'd stick close to the mine."

He set his chin on her shoulder, and for a long time, Dillon remained quiet, simply rocking her in his arms. Then he stroked her long ivory hair from her face.

"Iron Feather brought you here," he said in a grave tone, heavy with responsibility. The warmth of his breath lingered on her cheek. "I don't know all the reasons yet. But I should have protected you." His chest swelled large against Tessa's back. "This will never happen again," he promised. "You're under *my* watch now—"

"You got that right!" a familiar voice barked.

Tessa's eyes fluttered, only to catch the hazy form of Nell standing at the threshold of a cabin door. As her vision gradually came into focus, she became aware that Nell was holding up the shredded remains of her tent. In her other hand was a half-chewed granola bar.

"I can't believe you let her sleep outside, Dillon! You know damn well it's autumn and the bears are foraging before winter."

Tessa winced.

So the intruder had been a bear—

Drawn by the smell of her stupid granola bars. Chocolate-chip, no less! At that moment, she couldn't believe her own stupidity.

"I had no idea she was outside," Dillon snapped, refusing to loosen his hold on her. "I thought she was going back to your hotel. I paid for her room, remember?"

He nodded at a bow and a quiver of arrows on a table. "I was out hunting and returned after dark. When I heard gunfire, I grabbed my rifle and found her being attacked by a three-hundred-pound black bear."

Tessa squinted at Nell, her vision growing clearer now. She glanced around the cabin with old-fashioned chinking between its wide, rustic logs, spying a man's boots in the corner and a tall duster hanging on a wall. It was then she fully grasped that this was no dream—she was inside Dillon's home, perched on his bed. Only the soft bear hide separated their skin. When she began to comprehend that Dillon was stark naked as well, just like she was, a spike of heat burst on her forehead, pooling at her cheeks.

Nell, on the other hand, shook her head as though Dillon's bare form went with his eccentric frontier territory. She tossed Tessa's ruined tent into a trash can and folded her arms.

"Over my dead body is this young woman sleeping outside any more," she insisted. "Good thing I dropped by tonight to check on her, since she never came back to the hotel. Let me have a look at you, sweetie."

Nell headed over to the bed, averting her eyes from Dillon's bare skin and waving him to move aside like a fed up grandmother. With a dark look, he stood to his feet and wrapped himself in an old, red Navajo blanket that somehow made him appear taller. Nell ignored him and plopped next to Tessa on the bed.

"All right dear, I used to be a nurse long before I came to Colorado. So you listen and do what I say." She held up her index finger. "Can you follow my finger with your eyes?"

Tessa easily tracked Nell's finger swaying left and right. She held up two more fingers.

"How many fingers do you see now?"

"Three," replied Tessa.

"Can you tell me what day of the week it is? And the month?"

"Thursday," she affirmed. "It's October."

"Okay," Nell pressed, "repeat this series of numbers, only backwards: seven, two, eleven, fifty-three."

"Fifty-three, eleven, two, seven," finished Tessa quickly.

"Good. Now let's look at those lumps on your forehead." Nell gently pressed against her skin, massaging the bumps a little, but her fingers slid easily over the rest of Tessa's head where there were no swellings. "Do you hear ringing in your ears? Is your vision blurry at the edges?"

"Um, all of the above at first," she admitted. "But then, after—"

Tessa wanted to say Dillon's mysterious ritual, but she wasn't sure if she'd sound batty.

"I mean, after Dillon helped me out, the symptoms faded away."

Nell shot a glance at a jar on the nightstand that appeared to be filled with lard, yet reeked of herbs, pine, and rank animal fat. She gave him a reluctant nod.

"You're one mighty lucky lady that Dillon remembers his

mother's medicine." She carefully removed the bear hide from around Tessa. Nell's fingertips gently inspected the wounds on her back and shoulder, which no longer felt pain. "From what I can tell," she said, "these scratches are mostly on the surface. Fortunately for Dillon," she pointed at the vial of rubbing alcohol beside the jar on the nightstand, "he cleaned your wounds well. So he won't be in more trouble than he already is with me. But I have a job for you, young man."

Nell wrapped the bear hide around Tessa again and got up from the bed. She pointed a finger at him.

"You're going to let her sleep in this bed at night till she completely heals. Got that? Which puts you on the porch or in the barn, mister. And no more camping outside near the mine where any damn critter can rough her up. If it weren't for fall tourist season right now, I'd take care of her myself, so you'd better report to me each week on how she's doing. And for God's sake Dillon, don't let her take food anywhere close to that mine. Clear?"

Dillon's face remained stoic. Tessa wasn't sure, but she thought she detected a defiant look in his eyes as his jaw stiffened. She knew he was as stubborn as hell and not one to be pushed around easily, even by Nell playing nurse. But then that rare tenderness she'd spotted earlier snuck into the deep brown of his eyes. He cast a glance at Tessa on the bed, naked beneath the bear hide, her long blonde hair cascading over her shoulders. His eyes dropped to the wood floor, where her clothing lay in a heap. Beside her bloody shirt and ripped jeans was the white feather laced with bands of gray. Dillon picked it up, running his fingers over its soft edge.

When his gaze met Tessa's, his eyes were dark and intense

to a point that made her shiver. He held the feather out to her. Once she took it, without another word, Dillon gathered up her blood-stained clothes from the floor and threw them into a wood stove, closing the cast-iron door. The fire crackled and flared.

He turned to face the women.

"I protect what belongs to Iron Feather," he said in a voice that resonated deep within his chest. He glared at Nell like he'd just sworn an oath. Then he grabbed a pair of jeans and a camouflage shirt from a nearby dresser and handed them to Tessa. His gaze slid to an old, tintype photo on the wall in a vintage frame. Though the tall, Native American man surrounded by children in the image wore traditional attire mixed with a white man's coat from the nineteenth century, his long dark hair, razor-sharp cheekbones, and eyes the depth of night looked just like Dillon's.

Dillon nodded at the photo as though he'd heard it speak.

"Including her," he promised.

11

"You're marked now," Dillon told Tessa the moment the cabin door fell closed after Nell departed. "By the bear. They'll always hear you."

Tessa pulled the bear hide tighter around herself, trying to quell goosebumps. Holding up the camouflage shirt he'd loaned her, she gestured for him to turn around.

Dillon cocked his head. "It's not like anything I haven't seen before," he pointed out. "May I remind you that I'm the reason you didn't go into shock?"

She hesitated from unbuttoning the top of the shirt. "Um, thank you," she offered. "For whatever it was you did. I feel much better now, almost like it never happened." She swallowed hard, stumbling over her words. "B-But pardon me if I'm a bit spooked by your, uh, you know…"

"Ways?" finished Dillon. "My Apache mother's knowledge is why you're not in a hospital right now. And just so we're clear, staying here is not a luxury I normally extend to strangers."

"You think? With the way you greet everyone who comes by with a shotgun? It's a bit awkward for me too, okay?" she defended in a flinty tone. "Remember, I'm not the one who stripped *you* of your clothes without asking permission—"

A mischievous smile tugged at Dillon's lips. "Do you want to even the score?"

To her astonishment, he let the Navajo blanket fall to the floor and folded his arms.

"Happy to oblige."

His face held the casual air of a man accustomed to stripping down in hundreds of locker rooms before fights, regardless of the waterboys and journalists milling around.

Tessa was mesmerized—and pretty damn sure her jaw dropped at Dillon's raw, physical beauty. His body was sculpted beyond what most mortals could ever hope for from a mere gym. His was the kind of physique born of hard work and far too many fights, and from living off the land on a remote mountain ranch. Every muscle and sinew was tight and toned, his tan skin practically screaming for a woman's touch. Suddenly aware she was staring, Tessa caught herself and spun around, keeping her back to him as she threw on the long-sleeved, camouflage shirt he'd given her. When she stood up, the shirt draped to her thighs, making her look like she was wearing a minidress designed by the Mossy Oak brand. In spite of her acute self-consciousness, she began to laugh.

"Oh my God," she giggled, "I've been assimilated! I'm a Rocky Mountain chick—there's no going back now."

Dillon smirked, but it was no help to her at all—the

twinkle that lit up his eyes only made him more good looking and irresistible.

"Does this mean I'm going to have to outrun the wildlife?" she fretted, checking out the brown and gray leaf patterns on the shirt. "If I blend in too well with the forest, they might think I'm one of them."

"No, but you might need to outrun me," Dillon muttered under his breath. "It's not every day a looker like you is in my cabin. Wearing *my* shirt."

For the love of God, please stop! Tessa protested silently, hoping her words might somehow trickle into his brain. I know you're only teasing me. You're so damn handsome in your birthday suit, I can barely breathe or remember my name. And every time you smile, you take my breath away. Her cheeks flushed as she winced, knowing she couldn't afford to be hijacked by her emotions when she'd sacrificed so much to start over.

"Tessa," he studied her for a moment, his elongated pause making her even more uncomfortable, "I realize you're still adjusting here. This is a whole different world for you."

No shit, Sherlock! she thought. Does he have to constantly expose my inadequacies about the wilderness, when all I need is some wiggle room for my learning curve?

And of all things, there it was again. That infernal tenderness in his eyes that she didn't need by a long shot. He seems to reserve it for just the right moment to pierce my heart, she thought, feeling raw. What woman can resist a guy like this? He's thoughtful, drop-dead gorgeous, and he actually saved me from a bear—

"Well, it would help a *lot* if you'd put some clothes on!" she finally burst, trying hard not to sound too much like a prim school girl. "It's not that I'm against nudity. It's that, um, we barely know each other—"

"Actually, I believe we've gotten to know each other *bare* rather well."

Dillon grinned like the devil, sending her entire face into crimson heat. Nevertheless, he picked up his Navajo blanket from the floor and swung it around his tall frame without a hint of modesty. "Don't forget what Nell said," he reminded her, adding a patient timbre to his voice. "Somebody has to look after you. You endured a wild animal attack. And you have no wilderness training or mining experience to rely on, which is a pretty big recipe for—"

"Trouble?" she cut in. "Okay, I get it," she sighed. "Screwing up does seem to be my specialty lately. But I think I can handle myself here once I'm given half a chance to learn the ropes."

Tessa shot him a confident look, knowing it was all bluff. From the bottom of her heart, she wished Dillon's voice didn't sound as low and soothing as an evening breeze, the kind that could wrap around you and make you feel more whole. And she wished even harder that his tough yet caring spirit wouldn't get under her skin any further than it already had. Because the last thing she needed was another man who tried to own her—and who ended up diverting her from her true path.

"There's one thing I want you to know, Tessa," he said softly.

Despite her best efforts to tune him out, Dillon's voice felt to Tessa like a long hoped-for caress.

Without warning, he fell quiet again. His deep brown eyes locked on her with a focus that became excruciating. No amount of time that passed made him fill the empty gap with words. He appeared to be utterly comfortable appraising her, as though in his silence he could sense all the contours and shadows of her spirit. His eyes were so absorbing that she felt her pulse quicken, trying to fight off fleeting thoughts that seemed determined to remind her of how good looking he is.

"Nell and I have seen your courage first-hand," he finally said, his voice low and resonant. "She's a damn sharp judge of character. Quite frankly, so am I. And we're both onto your secret. You're tougher than you look, city girl. That bear attack alone would've made most people beg Nell to take them to the airport tonight to catch the first flight out of Colorado. But you're still here. It's no accident Iron Feather brought you to Bandits Hollow. I don't argue with his reasons."

Dillon paused for a moment, his eyes becoming even more intense. "Nell and I...we believe in you."

Dillon's words sucked the air from her lungs. She had no idea when she bolted from New York that she was heading into a wild and reckless territory—one where she'd be made to feel tested and vulnerable at every turn. She only hoped she really *was* strong enough to make it, both as a miner and as a woman who wouldn't lose herself too easily to the likes of Dillon Iron Feather. Squaring her shoulders, she lifted her gaze to meet his.

"Then I want you to tell me something, Dillon."

He simply raised his chin.

"What did you mean when you said the bears will hear me now? And I'll protect the stones?" she asked. "I hate to break the news to you, but I don't have a drop of Native American blood in me. As far as I know, I'm Irish and Scottish—"

Dillon stepped forward and leaned into her ear. "The spirits only judge the heart."

Tessa darted her gaze to the golden flames in the wood stove that were erasing her former clothes—her former life—to ash. She shook her head.

"I don't understand a damn thing you're talking about, Dillon Iron Feather."

"I know," he replied. He glanced one more time at the tintype image of his ancestor on the wall.

"Believe me, I know."

Tessa slept hard for the rest of the night in the comfort of Dillon's bed, her dreams littered with hazy images of stars, feathers, bears. When she awoke, she was startled to find Dillon lying on the floor by the bed in jeans and a green waffle shirt, covered only in the red Navajo blanket. She thought he'd headed to the barn last night. But obviously, he'd returned, almost like he was…protecting her? He reclined against an old-fashioned pillow made of blue ticking, his face in the throes of sleep, lost to dreams. His expression appeared softer than she'd ever seen before, no longer marked by the usual hard edges, but rather a stillness that seemed downright…

Vulnerable.

Tessa stretched out her arms and sat up cross-legged on the bed, enjoying the luxury of watching him in silence, the way she'd often caught him doing to her. Of course, his rugged features were enough to transfix anyone, but what intrigued her more was this rare chance, without his normal defenses in place, to perhaps peer into his…

Soul.

"Who are you, Dillon Iron Feather?" she whispered under her breath, her eyes tracing his lush dark eyelashes, rough-cut cheekbones, and jaw that for once didn't seem set against the world in defiance. "You're so handsome it hurts. Have you ever loved anyone—a girlfriend, maybe?" She'd already noticed he didn't wear a ring. And when she glanced around the cabin to check for evidence of a woman's influence, the humble place appeared as spare and unsentimental as possible. He didn't even show off any awards or mementos from his fighting career. From the looks of it, his cabin was every inch the rustic bachelor pad.

Tessa shifted awkwardly, drawing the faded quilt bedspread around herself that looked like it had been sewn a hundred years ago. "You know, it's okay if you haven't exactly been lucky in love," she admitted. "Some of the rest of us have struck out in that arena, too."

She sighed, recalling a few art school boyfriends who petered out fast, as soon as they discovered she didn't come from money. The urge to "marry up" was particularly strong in New York where the rents were sky high. And heaven knows, most of the male art students expected their girlfriends to babysit their careers and pay the bills while they became stars. Tessa secretly loved it that Dillon was a self-made man who refused to depend on anybody to secure his fate. Yet one thing about him continued to bug her, especially after what Nell had said of the Iron Feather brothers.

"Is it the anger inside from reform school that made you fight all those years? Or was it from losing your parents?" She observed the scars on his hands again, matched by the ones on his jaw. A shiver worked up her spine. "Because that anger sure can scare the hell out of the rest of us sometimes."

Dillon's dark hair was draped over his left shoulder and cheek like a thick curtain, hiding a part of his face from view. Tessa yearned to extend her fingers and draw his hair back to see him fully, wondering if it might enable her to peek into his secrets, too. Could she take the pain he'd buried inside that made his heart rage like a hot furnace? She found herself reaching for him in the air, only to snap her fingers back. She knew too well how fast his reflexes were, and that such an impulse could prove...

Deadly.

With a sigh, she scanned the log walls, clearly hewed by hand a century ago, for intriguing glimpses into his personality. Near the bed was a cast-iron wood stove, a gun rack in the corner, an old bathtub with potted plants inside beneath a window, and a small rustic kitchen by the front door. Few adornments lined the cabin but for animal hides, antlers, and Native American blankets. *This is a man who likes things simple,* she surmised. *Pure and close to the earth.* Aside from the vintage picture of Iron Feather by the wood stove, the only other decoration was a photo in a pine frame on a dresser, which she presumed was his mother before the accident. From her long dark hair like Dillon's, Tessa could tell she was Apache, as he'd mentioned. But in her eyes was a twinkle of delight for her three school-age boys that she hugged in her arms, which practically exuded joy. Tessa stared at her for a long time, feeling uplifted by the woman's abundant spirit. She spied Dillon in the photo, the tallest boy in the middle with hair to his waist, grinning like it was the best day on earth. Barrett was on the left, a bit shorter, with dark hair cropped like he wore it now. And on the right was a boy who had surprisingly fair skin and blonde hair as long as Dillon's, his only resemblance to his family being a square jaw and a tightly-muscled frame. "That must be Lander," she nodded, noting the intense look in his eyes. It was then her gaze fell upon an old turquoise pouch by the photo on the dresser.

Intrigued, she got off the bed and tiptoed to the dresser. She ran her fingers over the suede pouch that was faded and soiled in places, worn smooth and glossy at the edges. Sneaking a peek back at Dillon, who appeared sound asleep, she loosened the leather strand that tied the top and peered inside. There, she found dried herbs, strips of rawhide with curious markings, and an assortment of stones she recognized as topaz, opal, and sapphire. Tessa pulled out a piece of aquamarine and held it in her hand. A tingling sensation erupted over her skin along with warmth. Was it her nerves from looking at Dillon's things, or some kind of magic? Surely this pouch belonged to his ancestor, she thought, from the weathered look of the suede. Anxious, she stuffed the stone back inside, when she heard her stomach growl loud enough to make her jump.

"Hungry?" Dillon mentioned from the floor.

Tessa turned on her heels, cheeks flushed. She rubbed her hands together, trying to get rid of the tingling sensation, but it didn't work.

He rolled onto his side and perched on an elbow, his luxurious hair falling to the floor. He gave her a drowsy smile.

Wow, she thought. Nothing good can come from being *that* handsome at the crack of dawn.

"Um, sure!" Tessa chirped, stepping in front of the pouch so he wouldn't suspect she'd been handling it. "And I'm happy to help with breakfast. Just point me to the nearest pancake mix—"

"I don't eat processed foods," Dillon quipped. "Including pancake mix or your store-bought granola bars. That's for city folk—and bears, apparently."

"Then what do you eat?"

"Well," he stood up and headed to the kitchen to grab a large, steel pot. "If you take this to the creek outside and fetch us some water to boil, I'll have breakfast going when you come back."

"Hmm," she shrugged. She couldn't see why not, if she wore her jacket and remembered not to tote granola bars that might attract predators. "Okay." She went to slip on Dillon's jeans that he'd left for her at the foot of the bed and rolled up the legs nearly a foot to make them more suitable for her height. The fabric buckled loose at her small waist but ran tight over her ample hips, so she was assured the pants wouldn't slide off. "But as long as we're naming food restrictions," she added, "I want you to know that I don't eat badger, or possum, or whatever else it is you hunt around here."

Dillon smirked with the kind of amusement that came more from beholding Tessa in the soft, early morning light than her attempt at a joke. His gaze boldly traced over her rosy cheeks, slim nose, and heart-shaped chin before roaming to where her clothing stretched snug over her full breasts and hips. Goosebumps traveled over her body—never before had she seen a man look at her quite that way. It wasn't the possessive glare she hated from her former boss. It was pure…

Admiration.

Dillon lifted his attention to her blue-green eyes. "Don't worry about breakfast," he assured her in a deep voice she found unbearably sexy. "I won't serve you anything I wouldn't eat myself. You might be surprised by trying something new."

How can he possibly sound so alluring at daybreak? Tessa warred within herself, slanting her gaze to a window that faced the open door of the barn. From a high rafter hung the carcass of a bear. The black fur on its hide glistened in the sunlight, and a bucket was perched on the barn floor to catch the pool of the animal's blood.

"Small comfort, Dillon," she wisecracked, trying to disguise the fact that she was shaken by the sight of the bear. "If worst comes to worst, I might have to hitch a ride to town to get Nell's pancakes."

"Water," Dillon commanded, not having any of it. He held out the pot until she took it. "The first thing we need is water. All the rest is negotiable. And Tessa—"

"Yes?" she glanced at him.

"Don't ever let me catch you touching my ancestor's pouch again."

His gaze bored into hers while she stood speechless, wishing she could hide in a hole in the ground. What made things worse was that for a moment, Dillon seemed to enjoy the embarrassment that burned through her cheeks. His lips curled and his eyes sparkled, just like his mother in the photo on the dresser. She dropped her gaze and swiftly hustled to the door, when she felt his hand on her shoulder.

"Oh, and I forgot to thank you," he said in a wry tone. "I'm flattered you think I'm handsome in the morning."

12

Tessa wanted to die.

"I am in sooooo much trouble," she groaned, watching the creek water flow steadily near the cabin. She stared at her wavy reflection with furrowed brows that made her face look more confused. "Dillon is frighteningly attractive. Any fool can see that. And dammit, I need him to succeed out here. But get real—from what I can tell, he's half sensitive Adonis and half sociopath."

She threw back her head and cringed. "This is a recipe for disaster! How am I going to survive till I'm done with the mine?"

At that moment, a pine jay squawked, startling her. She gazed at the pesky bird on a branch in a tree. "Didn't you get any granola bars last night? The stash in my backpack was big enough to feed a small army."

She glanced at the spot where her tent had been, and all at once she realized that wild animals had torn apart her luggage last night, too. Clothing and toiletries were strewn in ruins across the frosty meadow.

"Terrific!" She threw up her hands. "Now I have to rely on Dillon for clothes as well. Is the universe trying to torture me?"

The pine jay screeched at her, and she responded with a surly look. "Don't give me that," she warned, jabbing a finger at the bird. "You come already clothed in a down coat. Let's see you try to sleep in the same cabin as that guy without getting *your* feathers ruffled."

Tessa shook her head and kneeled by the creek bank, dipping her pot into the water. Pulling it out once it was full, however, was another matter. She clutched the steel handles with a firm grip, and at the count of three, bravely attempted to lift the pot with all her might. When she managed to raise it to the height of her waist, she felt immensely proud of herself, and took a hesitant step back.

Instantly, the gallons of water in the pot sloshed against the side in a wave action, knocking her off balance. Before she knew it, she began to teeter. Her ankle twisted on a soft patch of ground on the creek bank and she lost her footing. She fell with a loud smack into the creek.

The groan released from her lungs rumbled over the water.

"Ugh!" she heaved, frozen to the bone. She was soaked through to the skin, and her hands were so cold when she tried to crawl over the rocks to the pot that her fingers ached like they were broken. On her hands and knees, she reached out her arm and nearly grabbed a pot handle when a rock dislodged and sent the pot floating downstream.

"No!" Tessa yelped, rising to her feet to run after the pot. Her sneakers made big sloshing sounds as she charged through cold water. She wanted to damn that pot all to hell, let it disappear down river, but she couldn't bear the thought of facing Dillon as some kind of wimp. No—I may have totally embarrassed myself in front of him this morning, she thought, but I refuse to keep looking like a rookie. Harnessing her willpower, she continued after the pot, dodging the largest of the slippery rocks, when she finally spied her chance. The pot had gotten stuck on a particularly jagged stone, and she dove for it, feeling triumphant. That is, until her foot wobbled on another slick stone that sent her flying.

Tessa met the cold water with a huge splash, her cheek mashing onto a rock. The stream continued to flow around her carrying chunks of ice. She was so cold she couldn't feel anything anymore, and she was surprised when she became aware that her body seemed to be rising to a standing position.

Before her was Dillon.

His dark eyes appeared concerned. And he'd put on strange clothes—

He wasn't wearing the waffle shirt and jeans he'd had on in the cabin. On his tall frame was a long, black wool coat with brass buttons, and his legs were clothed in deerskin pants. For some reason, his ankle-height moccasins in the stream didn't look soaked.

"You all right, *shich'choonii?*"

He braced her shoulders so she wouldn't fall again. His large hands felt oddly warm, even through her sopping-wet down jacket.

"It is *goosk'aas.*"

Tessa blinked a few times, unsure what he meant.

"Cold," he insisted, his lips stretching into a slight smile.

She looked down at her hopelessly wet clothes and nodded.

"No," he shook his head and pointed at the cabin.

"Him. He has been cold for too long. The power of Big *Yi'yee* is strong in him. He must learn to use that power to heal. You think you need him. It is he who needs you. To hear the stones again. They will protect you."

With that, he lifted up a turquoise pouch made of suede—the same one she'd toyed with on the dresser in the cabin. He opened it up and pulled out a hunk of turquoise from within and held it in his palm. It looked to her like the one Iron Feather had willed to Dillon. He nodded at her to indicate she should take it.

Hesitantly, she reached her fingers for the stone, which felt strangely warm like his hands, and she saw him crack a smile. His teeth weren't like Dillon's at all—they were large and uneven. Then she spotted a heavy scar across his cheek that she hadn't noticed before. It looked like it came from a knife fight long ago. Her attention only made him laugh.

"Mine the heart," he said.

The sound of his laughter floated over the stream like rushing water. All at once, his eyes began to turn round and yellow, frightening the stuffing out of her. His black hair frosted to the color of white, brindled with bands of gray, as he faded from her view. In his place rose a great horned owl that lifted its wide wings in the air. As it soared over the stream, its wings flapped with an eerie silence until it vanished into the darkness of the trees.

"Mine the heart," she heard his words echo over the water. "The stones will protect you."

Tessa gasped and looked down at her hand. No longer was there a piece of turquoise in her palm, but instead, a long white feather.

She clutched it against her chest, too petrified to move. Gulping down big breaths, she turned toward the warm light that streamed from the cabin windows.

And began to run.

"What happened to you?"

Dillon was at Tessa's side in a shot. He closed the cabin door behind her. The room smelled of sumptuous sausage and hash browns cooking on the stove. Even so, she buried her head in her hands.

"I-I think I saw him," she muttered, trembling all over. Her hands were lead weights and she couldn't feel a thing through her fingertips.

"Who? Bill Crouch?" Dillon eyed a rifle on his gun rack. "I've a mind to let him know the hard way never to set foot near my property again—"

"No!" She pulled her hands from her eyes and stared at Dillon. She tried to stroke her finger along his cheek, but she was too numb to detect its smoothness. Yet she was right—he had no scar there at all, like she'd seen only minutes before.

Because he wasn't the same man...

"I-I saw Iron Feather."

She held up the great horned owl feather that had been left as a...

Gift?

Tessa caught the look on his face—

Dillon was stunned.

"W-What?" He gasped, staring at the feather in disbelief. He blinked several times, suddenly registering that she was dripping wet. "Wait—you're shaking!"

In a flash, he scooped her up and carried her to a corner of the cabin. There, he set her on the wood floor and tore off her clothes with much less gentleness than the night before. "You could get hypothermia!" he burst, tossing off her shoes and socks.

Tessa wanted to crawl into a hole in the ground again, mortified that she was naked in front of him for the second time in only as many days. But she was so frozen her limbs refused to budge, no matter how much she tried to will them into action. Dillon left her side for a moment, and then to her astonishment, he lifted her in his arms and carefully placed her in an old white bathtub with clawed feet beneath a window. She saw pots of herbs nearby, the ones that had been in the tub recently where the plants could receive enough light. Then Dillon went to a closet to grab a heap of blankets. Swiftly, he covered her in thick layers of army wool and old quilts, tucking them around her body and beneath her chin. "Wait here!" he commanded before he dashed to the cabin door and disappeared outside.

When he returned, he had the steel pot in his hands filled to the brim with water. He set it on the wood stove where the fire continued to burn brightly. Rummaging in the kitchen for extra pots, he bolted outside and returned with more water. By the time he came back with the fourth large pot, he set it on the propane stove in the kitchen and turned the burner on high.

"Don't close your eyes—don't!" he instructed her. Trembling hard against the old blankets, Tessa felt like she'd turned into a human popsicle. To her surprise, Dillon laid down beside her in the big bathtub, encasing her in his arms. He held her close and pressed his face against her cheek. "It'll only be a few more minutes," he promised. "Don't fall asleep! Here, sing a song, any song—"

"I c-can't think of one right now!" Tessa growled, her voice shaky.

"She'll be coming 'round the mountain when she comes," Dillon sang.

"Sh-she'll be coming 'round the mountain when she comes. She'll be coming 'round the mountain…sh-she'll be…"

Tessa's voice drifted off, and Dillon shook her.

"She'll be coming 'round the mountain!" he cried. "She'll be coming 'round the mountain when she comes. She'll be driving six white horses—come on, Tessa!" he cried. "Sing!"

He patted her cheeks, and Tessa's eyes fluttered open. Dutifully, she sang round after round, until they came to the last verse.

"She'll be wearing red pajamas when she comes, she'll be wearing red pajamas when—"

Tessa burst out laughing.

"Red pajamas? What the hell does that mean?" The blankets shook with her giggles. "Who on earth wears red pajamas while driving six white horses?"

Dillon's eyes gleamed, clearly relieved she had enough gumption now to argue with him over the lyrics. "Well," he replied matter-of-factly, "in gold country, I imagine that means she was a hooker."

"Oh!" Tessa's eyes popped at the interpretation of the old song. "I-I had no idea."

Dillon's gaze swept her face, confident she'd stay alert now, and he brushed the soaking wet hair from her forehead before lifting himself from the tub. Heading to the stove, he hoisted up the large pot by the handles and carried it to the bathtub. Then he yanked the damp blankets from her body and slowly poured the water beside her.

Tessa yowled like a wild cat.

The warmth next to her skin was painful, though the water wasn't close to boiling. She'd gotten so cold outside that any rise in temperature felt scalding.

"It's okay—it's okay," he murmured in a soothing tone. He returned to the kitchen to fetch another large pot and poured the water in the tub, then bent to his knees on the floor. Cupping his hands in the bathwater, he trickled its warmth over her face, gently wiping the liquid over her forehead and cheeks. He dribbled water over her collar bone and chest. The liquid streamed over her breasts and pooled at her stomach. Dillon funneled more handfuls until it ran down her hips and thighs.

Tessa blinked several times, slowly feeling like she was coming back to life.

Dillon left her side and brought over another pot from the wood stove, cautiously pouring it over her entire body and watching as she eased down into its warmth. He retrieved one more pot from the kitchen and kneeled to fill the tub until she was submerged to her neck. She allowed her eyes to fall closed, letting the last remnants of cold release from her skin.

"City girl," she heard him whisper, as much to himself as to her. "How am I supposed to keep you safe, when every time I turn around you're in a fix?"

Tessa opened her eyes a little. His gaze was filled with such sharp concern it struck her to the heart.

"Don't worry," she muttered to ease his fears. "He gave me his medicine feather."

She spied the feather floating in the water by her foot, where she must have dropped it when he placed her in the tub. She fished it from the water and held it up to him.

"See? Iron Feather said the stones would protect us. If we listen to them."

The way Dillon narrowed his eyes, as though she might still be delirious from the cold, left her unsettled. Chewing her lip, she searched her mind for a way to supply proof.

"He called you Big *Yi'yee*," she remembered. "I mean, he said that influence is strong in you." She folded her arms over her chest to feel less self-conscious. "Dillon," she pressed, "you know full well I've never learned a single word of Apache in my life."

His brown eyes grew wide. All at once, Dillon's face was filled with an awe that made him appear softer than he normally allowed others to witness.

Speechless, he stole a glance at the turquoise pouch on his dresser and returned his gaze to Tessa. No longer did his features appear rough, as though the walls around his heart had somehow lifted a little. She wondered if this was what he was like before reform school, when he was young and his mother spoke of his ancestor's wisdom—and he believed her. The peculiar softness that claimed Dillon's face was so open it overwhelmed her.

With all of her being, she wished she could preserve that look. To capture the wonder Dillon must have known—and surely she had known once, too—before life's losses had left so many scars. To her surprise, she couldn't help herself. She leaned forward against the rim of the tub, bare skin dripping on the wood floorboards, her lips a mere inch from Dillon's—

And swiped a kiss.

When she gently pulled back, her wet fingers pressed against his smooth cheek. Dillon remained stone still, eyes closed, as though something unusual and perhaps sacred had happened. With the feather in her grip, Tessa ran it along the sharp edges of his cheek and jaw. She lifted the feather to caress the strands of his long hair.

"Don't say a word," she insisted. She brushed the feather over his lashes to keep his eyes sealed.

Her lips met his again.

Despite her mind listing a hundred objections because she hardly knew this man, she hungrily savored the taste of his mouth that was tinged with salt and spices. Dillon tilted his head, his lips working gently on hers, when all at once he cupped her cheeks and fiercely drew her to him. Sparks ignited on her skin as his lips devoured her, building a fire in places she hadn't felt alive in ages. He ran his fingers tenderly through her wet hair and clutched her temples with a force that left her reeling. Breathless, they broke away, gasping, and she leaned her forehead against his.

"Thanks," she whispered. "for rescuing me…twice."

Tessa placed her finger over his lips. God almighty, she thought, he may be handsomer than should be street legal and muscled up to wazoo, but I don't want anything to spoil the sweetness of this moment—even if he is a stranger. Dillon slowly opened his eyes, his expression remaining tender. He placed his hand on her cheek, brushing his thumb over her ivory skin.

"My pleasure," he said quietly. His gaze roamed over the droplets of water on her nose and cheeks that shimmered in the sunlight, when a glint surfaced in his eyes. "You know, I have to admit, city girl," he said. "I'm starting to look forward to your disasters."

13

Tessa splashed him with a big wave of water.

"What are you implying," she scolded, holding back a giggle, "that I'm Calamity Tessa?"

Rather than laugh, Dillon simply remained seated beside the tub, his jeans dripping wet.

He didn't breathe a word.

In silence, he took in the way the morning rays caressed her wet skin. His gaze followed the glimmers of sunlight off the generous swells of her breasts and hips—the kind that made supermodels look like mere twelve-year-olds. In his eyes, each drop of water on her skin was a pearl, perfectly positioned to highlight her curves. Tessa blushed at his appreciation, unlike anything she'd experienced. His gaze appeared raw and uncalculating, struck by the sheer beauty before him. Dillon's eyes met hers with a longing pure enough to slice her heart.

This time, it was Tessa who abandoned the idea of being

modest. She slowly rose to her feet, feather in hand, basking in the warmth of a shaft of light that slanted through the cabin window. Her eyes locked on his.

"I hardly know you, Dillon Iron Feather." She raised her chin in challenge. "So I should probably go back to Nell's hotel."

"Why?" He searched her face, confused.

"Because," she chose her words carefully, "if you…want me…"

She hesitated, allowing the silence to hang between them in the steam of the bath water.

"Then we should probably date. You know, like normal people."

Dillon tilted his head. The way his intense brown eyes probed hers was downright unnerving. He crossed his arms and shook his head.

"I don't give a damn about anybody's normal. And I *don't* date."

"Then what do you do?" she countered. She stepped out of the tub and grabbed one of the blankets from the floor, wrapping it around herself.

Dillon stood to his feet, towering over her. He turned to head for the kitchen. Then he grabbed a skillet from the stove filled with sausage hash and opened a drawer to pull out a hot pad and two forks. Returning to Tessa, he settled the skillet on a small, nearby end table and speared a hunk of food. He lifted the fork to her lips.

"I provide."

His eyes absorbed her face in that moment, sending sparks skipping through her limbs. Unlike her boss and her string of flaky boyfriends over the years who either wanted to own her or use her, his expression spoke of something else. Something new—

And in that instant, Tessa understood he was intending a whole lot more than serving her breakfast.

If she accepted Dillon's food—

She would be accepting *him*.

Her mind warped into a tangle of conflicting thoughts. She knew she was insanely attracted to Dillon, or she wouldn't have impulsively given him those kisses. Hell, she could hardly keep from tearing off his clothes right now. Yet she also knew every time she'd yielded to a man, her life had turned upside down. They either chained her to *their* goals or tried to drain her bank account, making her spirit shrink and wasting the ideals she'd worked hard for.

"I-I didn't come to Bandits Hollow to get lost in a relationship," she broke in, hugging the blanket around herself tighter. "I came—"

"To create a new future?" Dillon arched a brow.

She detected a glimmer of pride in his eyes that she didn't quite know how to decipher.

Stop it! Tessa thought. The scent of his food wafting to her nose was heavenly, and she began to suspect he truly was the devil in disguise. It took everything she had not to dive for his morsel of breakfast while ripping off his waffle shirt and jeans.

To her relief, Dillon swallowed the chunk of food himself and licked his lips. Just when she allowed herself to relax her shoulders a little, he brazenly stole a kiss.

He cupped her neck as if she were something precious and pulled her into his chest, his mouth roaming hungrily over hers. Not with ownership, but with a pure desire that made electricity snap through her veins. When she broke free, he swept a lock of wayward hair from her forehead and studied her eyes.

"There's only one thing I want from you," he whispered.

She braced herself, praying she had a few crumbs of willpower left not to succumb completely to his charms. She watched as he stabbed his fork into the skillet for another hunk of hash. He lifted the fork, barely brushing the divine-smelling food against her lips.

"I want to watch you make jewelry."

"W-What?" she replied, embarrassed by the growl that issued from her stomach. "Why?"

Dillon's jaw twisted, as though it required enormous will power on his part not to strip off her blanket.

"Because," he paused, "I want to see your soul."

He set down the fork on the table and ran his hands over her temples, threading his fingers through her silky blonde hair.

"Dating is for wimps."

Tessa's breath caught in her throat. What on earth did he mean by that? Cautiously, she stood on her tiptoes to search his eyes.

There, she saw a battle-scarred man with steel resolve who fights for what he wants. And who doesn't give up until he gets it.

"From the first moment I saw you, I wanted you," Dillon said. "That's a fact, Tessa—and dating won't change a damn thing. Sometimes, when you see what you want, you just have to take it."

"So you aimed a shotgun at me—*and* pulled the trigger? I clearly remember crawling on my hands and knees on the road out there so I wouldn't get blasted."

Dillon held back a smile. "That was a warning shot fired in the air to scare you. And then you *bit* my hand. After that, you swiped my gun and aimed it at *me*. Doesn't that make us even?"

"Hmm, maybe," she cut him off, tapping her lip. "You did attempt to pay for my hotel room..."

"See, like I said. I provide."

"That's your idea of wooing women? Besides hog-tying them, of course. You try to buy them a room and a meal, and they're supposed to lose themselves over you?"

"I don't want you to lose anything. Ever again," he replied in a voice so low yet forceful she felt it thunder through her veins.

"Th-Then what do you want?" she pressed, trying to ignore his effect on her, the dizzying way her blood rushed from her head every time he looked at her with such intensity.

Dillon folded his large arms and nodded at the table. "For you to have breakfast, for starters. And then for you to show me how you imagine your jewelry into being. It's your passion—you've risked everything for it. I want to see that part of you."

Tessa's pulse began to race. He knew *exactly* how to get under her skin—by taking an interest in the creativity she lived for. But did that make him a lover, or just a new and improved user? How could she trust someone she'd known such a short time with that piece of her heart?

"Only on one condition," she stated.

"What's that?"

She took the feather and set it beside his ancestor's pouch on the dresser. For a long time, she stared at the two items like they were omens, refusing to give a damn about how uneasy that might make Dillon. When she finally turned around, her eyes shot him a warning.

"You go first." She glared at him. "Show me how you make a living. All of it, everything you pour your energy and passion into—and the secrets you keep that go along with it. Stuff that you've never shown another soul."

She nodded at his hunting knife on the wall by the kitchen. "And then you promise me with blood," she made a crisscross over her hand, "that you'll never mention a word to anyone about how I make my designs."

Dillon's eyes gleamed in approval—the same way they had when he admired her for pointing a gun at Bill Crouch.

"My my, Tessa Grove," he smirked. "You always pull off grit when people least expect it."

He went to the dresser and yanked out a dry pair of camouflage pants and a shirt for her to wear, then fished for socks. When he was satisfied with the clothing, he handed her the stack.

"C'mon, city girl. You're about to go hunting."

14

"Pemmican," Dillon stated, handing her the bag.

Tessa read the label on the shrink-wrapped brick of meat that featured Dillon's unique *Iron Feather Brothers* brand:

WILD KILL
All-natural game from the Colorado wilderness mixed with local herbs, berries, and spices.

"There's three varieties," he added. "Deer, bison, and elk."

"Elk?" she replied. "I don't think I've ever tried—"

"Yes you have. It was in the sausage hash you ate ten minutes ago."

Slapping her hand over her mouth, Tessa attempted to choke down her surprise. She'd finally gotten so hungry she'd relented and taken a few bites of Dillon's food. She had to admit it was crazy delicious, though probably the most exotic thing she'd ever encountered. Her mother was always short on money while she was growing up, so beyond the usual ground beef, the only time they got creative was a roast duck once for Christmas.

"Wow, I guess I should be grateful it wasn't bear," she mentioned, hoping he hadn't slipped it in there on the sly.

Dillon shook his head. "My mother's people, the Jicarilla Apache, never eat bear," he noted like a warning. "Bears are *sash*—special messengers of strength for us. But we will save the hide and claws."

"Claws?" A burning sensation raced up the scratches on Tessa's back. She realized then she wasn't entirely over the trauma of the attack, so she attempted to change the subject. "W-What do people use this pemmican stuff for, anyway? Camping?"

"No," Dillon replied. "It's too expensive for the average family. My *Wild Kill* brand is power food, part of a world-class training regime. I only sell it to top contenders in boxing, martial arts, and cage fighting. Champions who'd never dream of putting processed food in their bodies. Staying in top form is their religion, and they want their nutrition to have the correct…spirit."

Dillon motioned to the rugged peaks beyond the cabin window. "I seek out game the right way. In those mountains, in the tradition my mother taught me. There are many rituals to master," his gaze narrowed protectively, "which I *never* violate."

Tessa tilted her chin, in awe of the passion that brought a fire to Dillon's eyes. All at once, he seemed more like a devoted medicine man than an eccentric mountain man with the exacting way he spoke of his mother's tribal customs. This is everything to him, she marveled, detecting a deep well of pride behind his guarded expression. And he's actually opening up about it to me. Yet one detail left her confused. "You know, I thought dads are usually the ones who show their kids how to hunt. It was your mother?"

Dillon's eyes took on a faraway look, and Tessa hoped the memory wasn't too difficult for him. "My father was part Ute," he began cautiously, folding his arms. "But he looked white—blonde, like my brother Lander. It was my mother who was full-blood and grew up in the Apache Nation near Dulce, New Mexico. She understood the old ways."

He slid his gaze to an old rifle on the gun rack, and Tessa wondered if it was the first firearm he'd received as a kid.

"My father taught me to shoot when I turned nine. I was the oldest boy, and we didn't have much money growing up, so my parents wanted me to be self-sufficient and know how to survive. But my mother gave me lessons in how to listen to the animals. How to learn their ways and do things in harmony."

Tessa arched a brow, not quite sure of his meaning.

"When you honor the spirits of the animals and ask their permission," Dillon explained, "showing gratitude for what they give you, it brings you in balance with nature." He nodded at the package of pemmican. "That maximizes your strength."

"So," she searched for the words, "you're saying…people buy your products because they believe it holds some special kind of power? That it will give them an edge?"

"It's not superstition," Dillon said, his voice testy. "It's a way of relating to life. Keeping the flow of spirit pure and strong." His dark eyes challenged her with one of his intense stares that made Tessa want to take a step back.

"It worked for me," he contended.

From his incredibly ripped physique, not to mention notoriety in cage fighting, Tessa had to agree he had a point. One thing Dillon appeared to be very good at was knowing how to win.

"C'mon, I'll show you the ridge," he urged. "It's a part of the wilderness technically owned by Lander that no one ever goes to, because the footing's too rough for most hunters and ATVs. And, well, because of Lander."

"Lander?"

Dillon merely smiled.

"You'll see. The only way to get up there is on very tough horses or seasoned mules. Lander lets me hunt in that territory, and we share profits. I think you're gonna like the views."

D illon was right—

Every step Tessa's horse took in the rugged backcountry behind his cabin was utterly breathtaking with the fiery hues of autumn. She found herself clinging to the saddle horn with all her might as her horse's powerful legs drummed beneath her while they climbed the steep mountainsides. For most ordinary livestock, this trek would surely be exhausting, she thought. But her quarter horse named Charlie behaved as if it were a stroll in the park. She could feel his thick hindquarters working steadily beneath her legs, and she made a point to stroke his mane and give his neck an affectionate pat. After all, they'd been riding hard for nearly two hours, and though the animal seemed relaxed, his neck glistened with sweat. When they finally reached the top of a ridge, Tessa gently pulled back on the reins to make Charlie pause so she could take in the panoramic view. Everywhere she looked was brimming with white-capped mountains lit up by swaths of golden aspens and occasionally highlighted by the spiral of a golden eagle in flight. Even Charlie lifted his velvety nose in the air, taking a long, deep breath as though in reverence. He nickered softly at Dillon's horse and mule ahead of them.

Charlie was certainly the biggest horse Tessa had ever seen, let alone ridden—a jet black gelding with white legs as thick as tree trunks who calmly navigated the precarious trails that would make most city slickers fear for their lives. She got the impression that, though he was only five years old, Charlie was so well trained he'd follow Dillon like a dog, regardless of how bad a rider she was. The only horse she'd mounted in her life was an old gray led by a carnie at a summer fair on Long Island when she was seven. She felt grateful for Charlie's expert footing as they closed in on Dillon and his tall, fire-red chestnut named *Hayiitka*. The word meant sunrise in Apache, he said, and he toted a lead attached to a surly bay mule called Sourdough.

Despite the fact that Sourdough often swished his tail and threw a nasty kick at Charlie, Tessa could count on the experienced gelding to keep enough distance to avoid trouble. When Dillon pointed over his horse's head toward a dense cluster of pines, however, Charlie's ears perked up. Tessa could feel his skin quiver with excitement against her calves—he obviously knew something was about to happen before she did.

Dillon waved for her to bring her horse beside him, far enough in front of Sourdough to avoid injury. It didn't matter, because Charlie did so anyway, apparently accustomed to this drill.

"They're here," Dillon said.

"Who?" Tessa kept her voice low so she wouldn't disrupt the alpine silence.

"*Dzées*—the elk," he replied. "You may have heard them called *wapiti*, a Shawnee term. They move like shadows in the forest, and they know every hidden draw and gully for miles. Expert outfitters can go a whole weekend without seeing or hearing them."

"Then how do you know they're around?"

Dillon pointed to a nearby pine. A portion of the trunk was scraped raw to the tenderest part of the tree where amber sap seeped in small drips. Pieces of brown bark lay on the ground.

"That rubbing's fresh," he observed. "Light yellow before oxidation—within the last half hour. Bull elk rub trees with their antlers to stake territory and intimidate other bulls. I've been tracking their signs for the last couple of hours, and the herd is really close. All we need to do now is call the bull in."

Tessa shifted nervously in the saddle at the thought, her rear-end muscles aching already from the long ride. She watched Dillon reach into a saddle bag and pull out the strangest contraption she'd ever seen. It was a large antler with two prongs, like a giant slingshot. The center was covered in leather and stretched out in a V shape to connect the prongs. At its base, the antler bone had been whittled into a whistle. Dillon held the base to his lips and blew a few puffs. Then he gave a hard blow, working his lips carefully over the mouthpiece the way a musician plays a harmonica.

Out came peculiar tones at tremendous volume. First, there was a high-pitched whistle, reminiscent of a piccolo, ascending to a lofty note which echoed through the trees. The call rang through the surrounding terrain and became softer over the pines, giving it a haunting quality, like the ghost of an alpha elk from long ago. Dillon transformed the second call with his lips, making a deep, trumpeting tone that resounded over the earth. He finished with a few short barks.

"Okay, time to get ready," he said.

Dillon was off his horse in a leap, confidently dropping his reins and the lead line without bothering to tie up the horse or mule.

"Come on," he urged.

Feeling a bit unsure, Tessa tightened both fists around the saddle horn. Slowly, she lifted her right leg and swung it over Charlie, bringing it next to her left leg so she could stand in the stirrup. Drawing a deep breath, she attempted to hop down from the tall horse, but the distance made her stumble and fall, landing on her butt. Patient Charlie ignored her and remained in place, his long reins dragging in the dirt. When Tessa got up and dusted herself off, she could have sworn she heard the veteran horse sigh.

"Well, that was graceful!" She winced, shrugging her shoulders. "I didn't know riding required tumbling skills."

"It's okay." Dillon's jaw clenched to hold back a laugh. "Charlie's been trained to ground tie under any conditions." He craned his neck to peer around her, admiring her soiled bottom. "Besides," he remarked, "a little dirt looks good on you. Shows off your, um…assets."

Tessa rolled her eyes, but her breath hitched when she spied the appreciation that lingered in Dillon's gaze, which had yet to let go of her curves. Sinking her hands into her pockets, she distracted herself by regarding the horses. They stood to attention facing Dillon with their ears straight up as if ready to salute, without a soul reminding them to hold their ground.

"Wow, your horses are really well trained. Wait, what are you—"

Before Tessa could finish, Dillon started dousing her with liquid from a spray bottle. He made sure to dampen her entire body in a cloud before zapping her between the eyes.

"Stop!" She ducked and threw her arms over head. "Have you gone nuts? What is that stuff?"

Her outbursts failed to halt Dillon's aim, and he grabbed her arm to keep her from running. Irritated, she yanked the spray bottle from his hand and blasted him in the face.

"Thanks," he responded, to her surprise. "Now spray me all over."

With a wicked gleam in her eye, Tessa gave him a few more blasts to get even. A bemused smile tugged at her lips. "For the love of God, please don't tell me this is your idea of flirting. Shotguns, hog-tying, and now this?"

"If I wanted things to get frisky on a hunting trip," Dillon countered, "I'd rub cow scent all over you. But that can get a bit dangerous with bull elks around, if you know what I mean."

"Wh-Whoa!" Tessa stammered, holding up a firm hand. "Don't you *dare* even think about it—"

"No worries," he chuckled, tapping the bottle. "This liquid kills all human scent. That way the wildlife won't smell us coming, as long as we stay downwind and keep our voices low. Here, let me do the bottom of your shoes."

Grabbing her sneaker before Tessa could protest, he steadied her balance and gave her foot a dousing. When he finished with the other foot, Dillon had her do the same for him and tucked the bottle back into his saddle bag.

"Now for the fun part." A grin teased at his mouth.

"That wasn't the fun part? Oh boy, I can hardly wait—"

Tessa didn't get the chance to complete her sarcasm when Dillon slapped a handful of mud on her forehead.

"Ow, knock it off!" she barked, but it was no use. Dillon held her shoulder and smeared mud all over her face, paying special attention to her cheekbones, nose and chin. The mud oozed down her neck and chest, sinking into the camouflage shirt he'd made her wear and blending with the dirt-colored fabric. She glanced down at her camo pants, made of the same earth tones, and heaved a sigh. God almighty, she thought, I could roll in a pig sty right now and no one would be the wiser. And it's making me itch.

"Just you wait, Dillon Iron Feather!" Tessa snapped. In a flash, she'd scooped a handful of mud, lightly speckled with frost, and slung it as hard as she could at him. Rather than duck, he closed his eyes and let it smack him in the face.

"More!" he commanded. "We need our skin to be as hidden as possible."

"My pleasure!" she replied with another swing of cold mud. This one got him in the forehead with such a loud splat that Charlie turned his neck to look. Tessa giggled.

"This is fun!" She dug another palmful of mud and swung her arm windmill style, like a bad pitcher, and laid another one on him. Dillon squinted, trying not to smirk. He rubbed the mud over the rest of his face and neck.

"Wait, let me guess," Tessa said. "Next is the part where we grab leafy branches and glue them to our bodies with tree sap? You take this camouflage business rather seriously, you know."

Dillon's eyes glinted. "No branches today." He rubbed the mud off his hands and pointed at her feet. "But you might want to step out of that elk shit."

She gasped and leaped from her spot. Tessa lowered her gaze to the dark discs of poop, some flattened by her shoes. "Ew!" she burst, sliding her feet against the grass to wipe her soles.

"That's actually a good thing," Dillon said as he walked over to his horse. "Scent-wise, it's great cover."

"Of course you'd say that," she muttered under her breath, picking up a stick to scrape off the last remnants from her shoe. "I'm surprised you haven't bottled it as hunter's cologne already."

She watched Dillon remove an old rawhide quiver that had been tied to the back of his saddle. It was an artifact of extraordinary beauty, with mysterious faded symbols stained in red, yellow, and blue along the sides, edged at the top and bottom with fringe. Dillon took out a bow from the quiver that looked like it might have been fashioned a century ago, along with a handful of arrows. Each arrow was about three-feet long, with turkey feathers for fletching and an old-style arrowhead made of white flint, attached with sinew.

To Tessa's surprise, Dillon slung the quiver onto his back and, without saying a word, kneeled down to the grass. He bowed his head and closed his eyes. Slowly, he began whispering something she couldn't understand. Yet it in the pristine mountain silence, his behavior filled her with awe. After a long pause he nodded, as though assured he'd been heard by the object of his prayer. He returned to his feet.

Something about the sight of his quiet dignity pierced Tessa to the heart. For all of his tough defenses, she could tell his mother's traditions mattered deeply to him. After all, this hunting expedition would be far easier with a rifle, or even a modern bow. In the hush of the moment, on the frost-covered ridge with nothing between them and the brightening sun but a vast expanse of blue sky, Tessa couldn't bring herself to break the silence and ask Dillon about what he'd done. She simply let the moment be.

Nevertheless, a shiver worked through her being. Staring at Dillon with the old hunting tools in his hands, she had the distinct impression that the spirits of his ancestors might actually now be accompanying them on the trip.

"We always ask the game for their meat and honor them with gratitude," Dillon turned to her solemnly. "It's the ultimate sacrifice—the highest form of generosity. For that reason, we waste nothing and share what we bring home, using every part. You'd want the same if it were your life that had been yielded in the hunt."

Tessa was speechless, her mind blown. She'd never thought of it that way—that everything she eats had been a form of supreme kindness and sacrifice. The sincerity she detected in Dillon's eyes was about as far from her former boyfriends and her old boss as a person could get.

And it made her heart flutter.

"That fresh elk scat on the ground you accidentally stepped on means we're where we need to be," he nodded. "Since I've already bugled for the bull elk, he ought to be heading our way in a matter of minutes. We need to take our hunting position. Near that brush is a good spot."

"Seriously, hiding in the brush?" she said, worried about ticks and spiders. "You sure know how to show a city girl a good time—"

"That's not all I'd like to do with you in the brush."

Dillon regarded her with a twinkle in his eye.

"It is mating season, after all."

A flush spiked Tessa's cheeks, making the dried mud on her skin crumble. Did he *really* just say that? She bit the inside of her mouth to quell a response while her pulse climbed. More dirt flakes tumbled from her face, and she caught them in her hand, breaking them apart with her fingers. "Oh Dillon," she sighed, knowing mud brown wasn't exactly her color, "how on earth can you call anything about this situation sexy—"

To her astonishment, his eyes locked on hers.

He paused, comfortable as usual in one of those silences where she never knew what to expect next. She fidgeted self-consciously.

"You're *always* sexy," he declared.

Tessa sucked air—

It wasn't a joke, meant to point out how silly she looked draped in mud, a city girl wannabe way over her head in the wilderness. In fact, the longing in his big brown eyes took her breath away.

He's so gorgeous, she thought, no matter how much dirt adorns his face and body from a mud fight. And it blew her away that he was thinking the same thing about her—

Even with a primitive bow in his hand that made him appear more wild and dangerous than ever, part of her wanted to grab those arrows from him and snap them in half before jumping his bones. Who the hell cared about pemmican, anyway?

But the answer was: Dillon did.

A lot.

And he'd brought her along to show her things he said he'd never shared with another soul except his mother. Traditional customs that were sacred.

All at once, a call from a distant bull elk ripped through the air, its piercing tones soaring over the ridge. Tessa glanced at her feet.

"I-I guess we'd better get in position, like you said," she acknowledged, afraid to peer up at Dillon. Afraid to witness that soulful look in his eyes again that called to her as loudly as the wild elk. Is this what they mean by chemistry? she wondered, feeling tingles dance up and down her skin—and into places she tried desperately to ignore. Her body ached for him in a crazy, mixed-up way that defied logic. Are my hormones getting the best of me, she wondered, like the wildlife here?

Tessa had never felt so blindly attracted to someone before, and God knows there were risks. Risks of losing herself and making mistakes, of crashing and burning like she'd done too many times. Only to have to pick up the pieces of her life, alone.

Always alone—

Another elk call cut the air, making her pulse pound in her head. She rubbed her temples to ease the throb. When she glanced up, there was Dillon, standing right in front of her, tall and silent as the trees. She hadn't heard him step so close. He stared into her eyes, his long dark hair casually falling over his cheekbones and broad shoulders. Somehow, he seemed even wilder here in this element, like he might just take her and have his way without warning.

Goosebumps flashed over her skin, and it was all Tessa could do not to grab those chiseled cheekbones and bring his lips to hers. His searing brown eyes poured over her, and she could tell his temples were pulsing, too. With everything in her, she wanted to devour him with thoughtless abandon, run her hands through that hair and strip him naked, then roll him in the grass and get even more dirt on their skin.

Who's the prey and who's the predator now? Tessa thought, unable to stop imagining how delicious his lips would taste, regardless of the fact that they were flecked with mud. When she heard the bull elk call again, she had to shake her head as if banishing a spell.

"If-If we don't take cover," she mumbled, trying to clear

her mind and stay on track, "we're not going to have much success at hunting today."

Dillon remained quiet, as was his way. Yet he reached out his hand and delicately ran his fingers down a strand of her long blonde hair, his gaze not wavering for a second from her eyes. The slow manner in which he traced a lock of silky hair, lingering at the fulness of her cheek as if she were a rare treasure, was the single sexiest thing she'd ever seen a man do. A mere touch, a mere slide of fingertips, hesitating over her skin while she watched the stiff clench of his jaw and enormous restraint in his eyes, told her she was the most desirable creature he'd ever seen. Every part of her body flared to attention, sparks spiraling in delicate places, and it made her breath catch.

"That depends on how you define *success*," Dillon whispered, leaning close.

The warmth of his breath slipped over her cheek and lingered there, making her feel like he'd somehow sealed her spirit to his. For a brief moment, she had to wonder if that's what the peculiar symbols on his old quiver pointed to. The hunter and hunted locked together, bound as one in the play of life. But how do you avoid losing yourself in that transaction? Who decides which one's the predator and the prey? A strange headiness came over her mixed with a grounded sensation, as though she were tethered to the earth, which she'd never experienced before. For the life of her, Tessa wanted to ditch her circling questions and dive into this man's beautiful, toned body to find out exactly how sensitive his touch could be. Perhaps the heat of his skin and tight, thick muscles would hold all the answers—

But her thoughts were broken by the sound of a loud crash through the forest.

Before them, a mere ten yards away, stood a magnificent bull elk. His body steamed from exertion in the cold air. He lifted his head, glaring in their direction, before letting out a fierce snort.

He was furious.

15

The elk was easily five-feet tall at his massive shoulder, with six points on each side of his thick antlers that extended for a yard over his back, making the animal's presence tower at nearly nine feet. Tessa's jaw dropped at the sight, watching him strike the ground before he blew another angry huff, chest heaving. Oddly enough, his fiery gaze scanning the top of the ridge appeared to ignore the two of them, as long as they remained still.

That wasn't too hard for Tessa—

She was petrified.

"Bulls guard their harems from other bulls, ready for violent clashes," Dillon whispered in her ear. "If we don't make a move, he'll be more interested in finding that other bull he heard bugle from my whistle. He has to fight to keep his territory, and he knows it."

Tessa held her breath as Dillon slowly, almost imperceptibly, raised his bow to shoulder height and loaded an arrow. When the bull elk lifted his muzzle and issued a series of tense barks to the air, clouds of moisture escaping his nostrils, her heart raced out of control.

"When are you going to take aim?" she whispered desperately. "He could gore us any second—"

"Patience and precision," Dillon replied so softly she could barely hear him. "You have to have the strength for both, or you'll never be the victor. We only get one shot before he runs—possibly at us. The last thing you want is to wound an animal and make him angry. Say a prayer."

"For what, our lives?" she answered hoarsely.

"No. For *his*."

Tessa tried to swallow, but her throat had become sandpaper. As the bull elk's chest swelled and he issued a wild call that she could have sworn shook the nearby trees, she was ready to pray to anything. Dutifully, she did as Dillon asked, closing her eyes for a second and requesting that the animal surrender his spirit. She pledged to use the bounty wisely.

When she opened her eyes, Dillon was staring at the elk with a burning focus. His gaze centered on the animal's chest as though he had a secret scope in his eyes with invisible crosshairs, capable of tracking the animal's slightest move.

A gnat landed on Tessa's cheek, tickling her skin, and she absently slapped at it. Her motion made the elk startle. He dipped his head in their direction, and to her amazement, she saw him snarl, flashing his gums that were devoid of upper front teeth. Only a couple of thick canines appeared at the edges of his mouth. The bull elk snapped his lips.

"What's he doing?" she whispered.

"That's a threat posture," Dillon said. "He's showing his

tusks. Elk are the only animals in North America that have them besides walrus. Stay behind me; he's decided he doesn't like us here. And he's about to charge—"

Tessa ducked behind Dillon in panic. Yet she couldn't resist peering past his broad shoulders to see what the elk was going to do. The bull elk dipped his head again with an angry snort, when he heard a rustle from a nearby bush. To their amazement, the rack of a younger bull appeared over the brush. The competitor lifted his head and bugled a call to rivalry. The larger bull whipped his head around and took a step toward his opponent to size him up. Blowing out a furious breath, he exposed the side of his wide chest to Dillon.

And immediately dropped to the ground.

Tessa was shocked when she grasped the fact that Dillon had fired his arrow that fast, piercing both lungs and felling the great bull in one shot. His fall frightened the younger elk, who vanished into the woods with giant leaps before Tessa and Dillon could blink twice. She heard the gurgles of the fallen bull attempting to breathe, a sad series of knocks and rattles from deep within his chest. Death appeared to drape over the majestic creature like an unwelcome shroud.

Tears slipped from Tessa's eyes. She hadn't expected that reaction, but the animal was so beautiful she could hardly bear to see it pass. Dillon stepped toward the elk, his expression grave. A low groan issued from the animal as its eyes fell closed. Bending down beside it, Dillon placed his hand tenderly on the elk's head. His palm met no resistance, and his lips moved in quiet reverence. When he stood up, he bowed his head to the animal and pulled out a pistol from the waistband of his camo pants that Tessa didn't know he'd been carrying.

He fired a shot in the air, as if to announce the release of the bull elk's spirit.

Tessa hugged her arms around her waist. She thought she might break down in sobs, but all that came from her lips was a soft wail. She searched the animal's body, his mouth and nostrils, wondering if she might actually see his spirit rise from his flesh. A light mist collected around the elk's form. It could simply be the warmth of his warm body heating the frost on the grass, she thought, forcing down a lump in her throat. Or maybe it was more…

"Thank you," she muttered softly, hoping his spirit could hear. "M-May your journey be light."

Dillon's eyes arrested hers. He seemed to approve of her impulsive utterance.

"I fired the shot to warn the rest of the herd to stay away," he explained. "So we don't have to deal with another bull surprising us."

He proceeded to lay his bow down on the grass and pulled a hunting knife from a sheath on his belt. It looked old, its large blade made of black obsidian. Tessa figured he must be going to quarter the elk right now, while the meat was still fresh. Instead, he grasped one of the animal's long antlers and lifted his head. Setting the elk's chin on his knee, he opened its mouth and proceeded to carve out the two canine tusks with swift, efficient slices to the gums.

Fingers bloodied, Dillon closed his palm over the tusks and set the elk's head back down, letting go of the giant antler. He wiped his hunting knife on his pants and returned it to the sheath. When he looked up at Tessa, he stepped around the elk and walked to her, holding out his hand.

"These are for you."

Tessa's stomach did flip flops. Good God, she thought, gazing at the blood dripping from his palm. Is this Dillon's idea of a souvenir from our first wilderness date? The thick, rectangular tusks were covered in blood with pieces of the gums still clinging to them.

"They carry the energy of the bull's mighty spirit," he explained. "I want you to have them. To protect you in the future."

Dillon's eyes were filled with such deep conviction she couldn't bear to refuse him. As he pulled an old bandana from his back pocket and wrapped the bloody tusks inside, she winced, holding out her hands.

He put the bundle into her palms. Reverently, she tucked the bandana in her front pants pocket where it wouldn't fall out. Blood seeped against her hip, still warm from the elk's life. A tear trickled down her cheek.

Dillon wrapped his arms around her and held her close. She pressed her cheek to his hard chest, trying to remain strong. But she could feel her body trembling.

"It's okay," he whispered into her hair. "This was your first time. You'll never forget the magnificence of that bull elk's presence. When you do things the right way, their spirit will remain with you. Always."

"You lying piece of shit!" a voice called from the nearby trees.

Dillon and Tessa glanced up, spotting a man with long blonde hair astride a pinto horse galloping toward them in a frenzy. He held a cowboy hat in his hands, waving it up and down like a crazy man. Then he pointed it at them as if he intended to pummel them with it.

"I'm taking that meat, you asshole!" He brought his wild-eyed horse to a sliding stop in front of the elk and dismounted. Tossing aside the reins, he began to march toward them in a huff. "It's about goddamn time I had some fresh steak for dinner. And don't you *dare* lecture me with your Apache mumbo jumbo."

Dillon kept his arm around Tessa's shoulder, bolstering her stance. She half-wondered if it was to protect her from the Tasmanian Devil charging in their direction. Yet oddly enough, Dillon didn't seem terribly concerned.

"Tessa," he sighed, "welcome to the wild world of Lander." He gave a nod at the fuming figure stomping up to them with his fists clenched. "And you thought *I* was crazy."

16

"You're trespassing!" Lander insisted. "You're never supposed to hunt on my land without calling me first. You know the rules—my staff could've had you arrested for poaching. I bet Barrett would *love* to lock you up."

"What can I say. I forgot my cell phone," Dillon replied dryly.

"You probably don't have one, you big Sasquatch."

Tessa stepped back in shock as Lander dove for Dillon's legs, knocking him to the ground. The two began to wrestle hard on the grass, with Lander throwing savage punches that seemed to far outweigh Dillon's supposed infraction. When Lander rose up to drill his brother's gut, Dillon didn't bother to close his eyes, taking the slams with a tolerant expression. Lander kept flinging more abuse into his brother's tough abs until he was out of breath, becoming all the more angry when he saw Dillon smirk. He finally rolled off his brother, chest heaving, when he glanced up and noticed Tessa. Stumbling to his knees, Lander regained his feet. He brushed himself off and gallantly extended a hand to her.

"Geez, Dillon!" He shook Tessa's hand so vigorously she thought her arm might drop off. "Where on earth did you find this bombshell?" He flashed her a sly grin. "Hi, I'm Lander—the better-looking brother. Do you need help, sweetheart? An escape from Dillon's backwoods hell, maybe?"

Lander yanked a cell phone from his pocket and held it up. "I can get my man to fetch the limo back at the ranch. You must be awful tired," he scanned her muddy clothes, admiring her curves, "and in need of a bath, I might add." He glared at Dillon. "Is this some kind of excuse for a mating ritual? You need to get with the times, bro. No wonder women run from you screaming."

Lander dug into his jeans and handed Tessa a small set of binoculars. Smiling, he pointed to a distant hill beyond the ridge. "Picture the good life, sweetheart," he said, "just waiting for you."

Confused, Tessa lifted the binoculars to appease him, peering through the lenses. She spied a timber mansion the size of a hotel, with thick wood beams and river rock accents to set off its palatial architecture. It was so beautiful, she had to bite the insides of her mouth to prevent herself from gasping. A black limousine was parked in front in a circular driveway, and there were several guesthouses nearby that were larger than most homes she'd ever seen. Scanning the massive ranch, she identified two huge barns and acres of corrals that served as a livestock operation, along with an air strip for a private plane that featured an *Iron Feather Brothers* logo on its tail.

Tessa's mouth dropped. With all of the hunting excitement, she hadn't considered what was beyond the ridge, much less the notion that some millionaire lived there.

"Better yet," Lander decided, "I could have Roger bring the helicopter." He searched the grass on the ridge and motioned to a suitable flat spot. "He could land right there on that meadow, and you'd be at my place in a jiffy. Roger can land anywhere in a pinch—I stole him from the last president."

"P-President?" Tessa stammered. "Of what—some cattle company?"

"The U. S. of A!" Lander laughed. "Don't worry about a thing, darlin'," he assured her. "You say the word, and me and Roger will get you down from this ridge and treat you like a lady." He slanted a glance at his brother. "Which I'm sure you haven't experienced from Dillon."

Dumbfounded, Tessa checked Dillon's eyes. Lander's over-the-top grandiosity seemed downright certifiable. Could he really be the owner of that ranch—or was he delusional?

Dillon merely shrugged. "Tessa Grove, meet the infamous Lander Iron Feather. My," he gave a short sigh, "beloved brother."

"Wait, I never claimed you as a relation," Lander replied. "You don't have a lick of civilization in your whole body. And by the way, you smell like dead elk."

"I know," Dillon replied. "And if we weren't bound by blood already, I'd have killed you by now."

Lander thrust up his chin, squinting menacingly, but Tessa noticed he inched a step back. Despite his bravado, he knew better than to mess too much with Dillon.

"Okay, Mister Blood Bath. Can't you pack soap or something on these trips? You're a mess! I heard Ralph Lauren's staff builds makeshift showers in the backcountry of his spread. You can afford to do the same, if you gave a shit." Lander shook his head and turned to Tessa. "Don't let this Neanderthal fool you. He may be scruffy, and a stain on our family's reputation, but he's a fricking genius. Why he runs around like a mountain man is beyond me. That meat business of his filled a hole in the market that nobody saw coming. Who'd have thought you could make bank on jerky?"

"Pemmican," Dillon corrected. He rolled his eyes at his brother. "And if it makes you feel any better, you can take the bull elk today since I forgot to call you. You and your men can cut up all the meat you want, as long as you promise not to waste anything and pack out the rest. Now if you don't mind, Tessa and I will head back to my cabin."

"That old thieves hide out? You gotta be kidding me! You don't even have electricity and running water. Listen honey," Lander put a thoughtful hand on Tessa's shoulder, then realized the fabric was stained with blood and pulled his fingers back. His rubbed his palms together. "I'll have my staff cut some fresh steaks and my chef Francois can marinate them however you like. You let me know what evening you two can dine with us." He turned to Dillon. "Think you can manage a bath before then? Watch out, Miss—Bigfoot here may pretend to be close to nature, like our ancestor Iron Feather. But that don't mean he ain't no goddamn millionaire—"

"Lander!" Dillon growled a warning.

Tessa stumbled a couple of steps away from the two men, stunned. She felt like she'd been slapped in the face.

Millionaire?

Could he be serious? Why hadn't Dillon told her? That he was actually...rich. Not some struggling ex-fighter living off the land. And why, oh why, did he reside in a backwoods cabin? Unless he was trying to fool stupid, naive women like her—

Heart drumming, Tessa's mind warred with a flurry of thoughts while she scrutinized Lander's expression. Though arrogant and far too impressed with his ranch and big boy toys, she could tell immediately that he wasn't lying.

When she glanced at Dillon, the rage in his eyes at his brother for letting the facts about their lives slip confirmed it was the truth.

Tessa felt like she'd taken a bullet to the gut.

She laid her hands on her knees and tried to catch her breath, her thoughts swirling.

Dillon darted to her side. When he grasped her elbow to give her support, she ripped her arm away.

"Well, learn something new about you every day, right?" Tessa glared at him, shocked he'd never bothered to let on. "Oh, don't worry. I'm sure it's all water under the bridge for a guy like you." She noted Dillon's hands. "Or blood, if that metaphor suits you better."

Tessa's eyes misted in fury. She backed up several strides, holding up her hand to warn the two men not to even think about following her.

"So, you're a couple of rich boys, huh? In some Fortune 500 business together? Wow, it must be fun to take unsuspecting women for rough rides in the woods. Quite the joke! I bet you have a great time laughing over whiskey about those dumb chicks who try to tough it out in the backcountry." She pointed at Lander's ranch. "Especially when you have a shiny new limo parked down there."

Though she was at the brink of tears, Tessa refused to be buffaloed any further by the likes of these two. Dammit, if I wanted to live in the lap of luxury, she thought, I could have hooked up with Arthur Jacquier long ago and been promoted to a higher salary—along with serving as his mistress. Money brought nothing, as far as Tessa was concerned, except exploitation and disrespect. Sure, her road to authenticity may have been rocky so far, but she wasn't about to trade it for a hollow life with the kinds of players who would never cherish her.

"Well, I'm not your fricking joke," Tessa spit out. "And I'm *not* for sale. I don't care how many private planes you two have, or how much money's in your bank accounts." She cast a disgusted glance at Dillon. "Of all people, you should have figured that out by now. Or I never would have opened that rickety mine on nothing but a dream. So you two stay back, and don't bother trying to keep your pretty little secrets from me anymore."

She turned and dashed down the ridge, running as fast as her legs could carry her. Dodging rocks and trees, she headed to where she remembered they'd left their horses. Tears streamed down her cheeks, which she hated herself for, angry she'd ever let Dillon under her skin. Tessa slapped the tears away.

"He's a fake!" she cried to the wind, wishing it could somehow carry her off. "And a liar! How could I have been so stupid? He was just toying with me in that stupid rustic cabin. Playing an elaborate game, like all men do."

Breathless, she finally found Charlie grazing in a meadow beside Dillon's horse and mule, not far from where they'd originally dismounted. She ran up to the gelding and hugged him like an old friend, tucking her face into his warm, soft mane. "Oh Charlie," she moaned, letting her sobs come freely now. "Oh Charlie." She twisted the horse's long mane with her fingers. "I came all the way to Colorado, risking everything, only to get duped by another user. Who thought he could fool me like all the rest. You're lucky you're a gelding, Charlie." She stroked his smooth, silky neck. "You don't have to worry about relationships."

Resting her head against his neck, she allowed the feel of his soft fur to comfort her a little, but she feared Dillon might catch up soon. "It's you and me, Charlie," she said, shoring up her nerve. She grabbed the reins from the ground and stuffed her left foot into the stirrup, reaching to grab the saddle horn. At the count of three, she hoisted herself into the saddle. "Think you can get me back to the cabin, buddy?" She squeezed his sides with her heels. "I promise, if I find any carrots in Dillon's kitchen, you'll be the first to get them before I leave his ass for good."

Charlie broke into a gallop at her urging, which scared Tessa to death, but not more than staying around Dillon Iron Feather. She clung to the saddle horn as if her life depended on it as the horse bounded down the mountainside. Trees whipped past them in a blur, and she had to shut her eyes and duck low at times to avoid branches. Her plan was to bolt to

Dillon's ranch as fast as possible, then call Nell to pick her up. But what would she do after that?

Seal my heart under lock and key, Tessa vowed to herself.

Her mind became a cauldron of plans. She could stay at Nell's hotel for a few months and work as a waitress, she figured. That would give her enough time to pull out as much turquoise from the mine as possible, carrying a gun if that's what it took to keep Dillon at bay. After all, it was her claim, her dream, and nobody could stop her from getting the raw stones she'd need to launch her own jewelry line. When she had enough stock to work with, she could move somewhere—anywhere—and set up shop, only returning when she needed more stones. Dammit, she'd mine at night with a hundred lanterns while Dillon was asleep, she resolved, if that's what it took to circumvent him.

Minutes passed, and though Charlie's gallop had begun to slow, they came upon a grove of aspens with low, thin branches that sliced at Tessa's face, forcing her to use her elbow to shield her eyes. By the time Charlie broke into a trot, she peeked over her sleeve, only to realize they weren't near Dillon's ranch at all. She didn't recognize the terrain anymore.

Tessa's heart began to palpitate, and she slowed Charlie to a walk. If she'd gotten them lost, what hope did she have to find her way back to civilization? She pulled her cell phone from her pocket, desperately tapping at an app for a map. There weren't enough bars to indicate a good enough signal. She glanced around, attempting to figure out the path to their original trail, when all at once, she heard the loud rumble of construction equipment. Curious, she urged Charlie in the direction of the noise, and they came upon the edge of a ridge, overlooking a wide river.

On the river bank was a yellow construction excavator, carving up loads of sandy soil next to the river. It dumped its bucket onto a huge platform connected to a machine that contained a large, rotating cylinder, which ground the debris and spit out water and rocks onto a conveyor belt. Pulling back the reins, Tessa brought Charlie to a halt.

Where on earth was she?

And what were these construction workers hoping to achieve?

She scanned beyond the river, but there were no ranches or buildings in sight, which she thought was odd for such a big operation. Yet the workers appeared to have been there for a while, because there were piles of river rock left by the water. Tessa heard the whistles of the men below, directing one another to move the excavator to another fresh spot for digging. Intrigued, she nudged Charlie for a closer look, but he stopped, spying a barbed-wire fence before she did. It appeared to be designed to keep snoops like her out.

"Gold," she heard a soft whisper from behind her. "They're placer mining for gold."

17

Tessa whipped around in the saddle. It was Dillon—
She hadn't heard his horse come near her through the brush. How was that possible? He'd snuck up on her like Iron Feather's ghost—

"Patience," Dillon reminded her. "And precision. There's a reason my ancestor was the best tracker in the West."

He jumped off *Hayiitka* and was at her side in a second, gripping Charlie's reins in his fist.

He simply gazed at Tessa.

Like she was his whole world...

For a long time, his silence did all the talking.

What she saw in his eyes was pain.

Sadness.

And a pierced longing.

Tessa refused to be fooled, however, no matter how sincere Dillon might appear. After all, she'd been duped by those big brown eyes before.

"You lied to me!" she seethed, trying to jerk the reins away. She kicked at Charlie and attempted to steer him with all her might. But it was clear he wasn't going to budge with his master holding him firm.

"I was an open book to you!" Tessa burst through gritted teeth. "You acted like you admired my integrity a few days ago. What was that—a ruse? Who the hell are you, Dillon Iron Feather?" Her hands balled into fists around the leather reins that did her no good. "Because quite frankly, I laid it all on the line when I came to Colorado, and didn't hide a damn thing from anybody. Too bad you don't have the same standards—"

"Tessa," he said softly, "we made an agreement. You wanted to take part in what I do by going hunting today. And allowing me to show you my mother's traditions. I've never done that with *anyone* before."

"Who gives a damn!" she retorted. "It's not your privilege to hold back big chunks about your life, Dillon, while you knew I was being completely honest. This happens to be why people date, by the way—to find out the truth about each other. And don't you dare come at me with your 'I take what I want' bullshit. I offered to go to Nell's, to not proceed this fast at all. But no, you wanted me to stay, making it sound like we were going to be perfectly honest with each other."

Dillon kept quiet, letting her fume and expel her emotions, which only made Tessa madder. When she was finally done with her fire-breathing arguments, he didn't utter a word. His stare was focused and all-consuming. No matter how angry she became, she couldn't get his beautiful eyes out of her mind, and that made her furious.

At wit's end, she ripped off a nearby aspen branch and

furiously whacked at Charlie's rump, hoping he might respond, but it was no use. The faithful gelding danced in place before his master.

"Tessa," Dillon implored, his voice as soft as velvet.

She closed her eyes to try and tune him out, kicking wildly. "C'mon, Charlie!" she begged, giving him another whack. "Let's go—"

"Tessa, don't leave. I care for you, more than I could ever imagine in such a short time. It's like my ancestor brought our hearts together on purpose."

Charlie fell still, despite her attempts to dig her heels into his sides.

"Stop!" she demanded. "I don't want to hear that." She threw her arm over her face so Dillon couldn't see her cry. Then she dropped her reins over Charlie's neck and pressed her palms over her eyes. "You lied to me," she repeated, exasperated. "I don't care how rich you are. *No one* gets to play around with the truth on me, ever. And you'll never own me, Dillon Iron Feather."

An owl hooted through the trees, startling them both. Its call echoed in the shadows of the woods, and Tessa peeled her fingers from her face to glance in the direction of the sound. All at once, Dillon swung himself onto Charlie's back behind her saddle. He grabbed her like he was never letting go.

"Tessa," he whispered, hugging her tight.

"Don't you dare call me city girl!" she warned through gritted teeth, tempted to bite his hand again. "I know so much more than you think, and I know exactly where crap like this leads. Now take me home."

Dillon leaned his head against her shoulder, pressing his warm cheek to hers.

"You *are* home. Here, with me. Don't you see that? I know it's fast and must feel crazy. But beautiful Tessa—didn't you realize I was going to tell you all those things today? It's only eleven o'clock in the fricking morning. And Lander with his big mouth beat me to it. Here," Dillon pulled an envelope from his pocket and handed it to her.

Tessa gulped a few breaths, wiping tears from her eyes to try and calm down. She didn't want to open his stupid letter—or give him any more chances, either. But the way she figured, with his iron arms around her in the saddle, she was stuck for now. Might as well get this over with, she thought, if it gets me back to the ranch faster.

She pulled out a letter from inside the envelope. In it was an order from some fancy training facility in Los Angeles—she could tell by the decorative logo with golden boxing gloves. Numbers filled grid marks on the page with requests for various varieties of pemmican and a total amount at the bottom.

It was a hundred-thousand dollars.

Tessa sucked air.

She sealed her lips, not wanting to reveal her astonishment to Dillon.

"Why are you showing this to me?" she whispered, frustrated. "You know I don't care—"

He squeezed her so tight she couldn't finish her sentence while Charlie dipped his head to calmly nibble grass.

"I brought this order to be transparent with you," he replied. "I know I live in humble circumstances—I do that on purpose. After my last fight, I wanted to figure out what's real and get my life back together, without all the glitz of the life I'd known in Las Vegas. I was going to give you this letter as soon as we'd packed home the elk. And then make you dinner tonight—with fresh steak."

"Why didn't you show this to me before?"

"Because it's not who I am. *This* is who I am."

He gestured at the golden aspens and rugged, snow-speckled mountains that peeked over the treeline. "This wilderness, the wildlife here, the kinship I have with it all that came from the soul of my mother's people. I wanted you to have a taste of why I really do this. Of my heart."

He brushed aside her hair from her cheek to look into her eyes. "Can't you see that, Tessa? The money's secondary for me. Imagine becoming famous on the fight circuit for all the wrong reasons, because you knocked some poor fool into a coma and half the country thinks he died. Then hauling in cash and celebrity as some kind of hero when it no longer means a damn thing to you. I wanted you to experience what *does* mean something to me—the kinds of things that last."

He grabbed Charlie's reins and guided the horse away from the lookout point over the placer mine. His horse and mule dutifully followed them. Then he grasped Tessa's chin and turned her face slightly so he could kiss her cheek. He bowed his forehead against hers.

"You've already stolen my heart, Tessa. Your guts, your passion…and your crazy beautiful curves." His eyes sparkled, watching hers brighten a little. "I'd ditch selling pemmican for the Iron Feather Brothers brand in a New York minute if I thought it was going to come between me and the people who matter. You can always make a buck, Tessa. But you can't always find a heart that fits yours. That kind of magic is...rare."

He reached up to stroke her cheek. "Besides, my brother's an asshole to work with, in case you haven't noticed."

"Yeah," Tessa's lips lifted into a smirk. "I did kinda get that impression."

A smile passed over Dillon's face, but then he became stern. "All I care about is passion, like the way you feel about your jewelry. As long as I can live a life I love. Especially with somebody like...you."

Tessa became silent. She felt she deserved this pause, after the many times Dillon had gone quiet on her and left her emotionally flailing, wondering what was on his mind. Finally, she drew a deep breath and cleared her throat.

"Then I have a question for you, Dillon Iron Feather," she said in a low, demanding tone, as though the future of their relationship hinged upon his answer. "What the hell would you know about a New York minute?"

Dillon laughed.

"Not a damn thing, to be honest. But I do know I want you like nothing I've ever wanted in my life before. And we have to get out of here, before we get shot."

He kicked Charlie. As the horse broke into a canter, Dillon whistled for *Hayiitka* and Sourdough to follow.

"What are you talking about?" Tessa stole a glance back at the construction vehicles behind them.

As soon as they were beyond another hill, Dillon urged Charlie into a full-blown gallop.

"Because," he shouted into Tessa's ear as the trees whipped

by, "something tells me that was Bill Crouch's dig back there. Illegal mining on BLM land. I'll tell Barrett to get the law on him as soon as we get back. But I'm pretty certain Crouch wouldn't want any witnesses around."

He tucked his chin against Tessa's shoulder, his body swaying with hers to the rhythm of Charlie's motion.

"Alive, that is."

18

Once they settled the animals in the barn, and afterwards headed to the creek to wash off their hands and faces, Dillon led the way to the cabin. He called Barrett to report their discovery of the illegal gold mining near Lander's property. Tessa, on the other hand, went straight for the bed and fell face forward, bouncing on the mattress. Every muscle in her body hurt after the ride up to the ridge and back that day, and she relished the softness of the old quilt and pillows against her skin. She thought Dillon might soon flop as well, because surely he was exhausted, too, but he lingered for a while in the kitchen. He came over to the bed and tapped her gently on the leg.

"Here," he said, "I want you to have this. You must be starving."

His pemmican sat on a china plate in his hand. Tessa's stomach was already making a ruckus, since it was nearly evening and they hadn't gotten dinner yet, but she wasn't at all certain about this backcountry fare. She sat up on the bed, eying the pemmican warily.

"Go ahead," he smiled, "it won't bite. And you might like it."

She squinted at the food. "Will it transform me into a champion or something?"

"Only if you train like hell. For years."

"I was afraid you'd say that," she confessed. She picked up the brick of meat, flecked with dried berries and bits of herbs, and took a nip. It was vaguely tasty, a peculiar combination of smoked wild game and sweet and salty flavors in that super-healthy-but-I'm-dying-for-a-Big-Mac kind of way. From the expectant gleam in Dillon's eyes, she could tell he was proud of his creation, waiting for her response. Yet she couldn't disguise the tension on her face as she struggled to swallow and put the odd flavors behind her. Crap, she thought, wish I had a shot of liquor to wash this down.

"You know, I'd never ask you to give up your pemmican business," Tessa pointed out, trying to hide her longing for the bottle of Cuervo she spied near the stove. "But do we have to share the same tastes?" She glanced down at her figure in the mud-stained camo clothes. "I know you don't do refined foods," her brows furrowed as she patted her chest and hips that appeared to be buried in fabric. "But with all this outdoor activity, I feel like I'm losing my curves. Don't you have any, um, biscuits? You know, yummy carbs?"

A grin teased at Dillon's lips.

"The last thing I want is for you to lose those curves. I'll make biscuits right now."

He grabbed a bag of blue corn flour in the kitchen and

opened the icebox to fetch eggs and a jar of milk that looked like they came from a nearby farm. After he'd put them in a bowl, he took down an old, Native American grinding stone and pestle from a shelf. Emptying pine nuts from a bag into the stone bowl, he began crushing them. When he finished, he poured the nut meal into the mixture along with salt and a dash of dried chili and baking powder. Then he brought out a tub of lard and scooped several spoonfuls into a cast-iron pan. Cranking open the kitchen window, he turned on the gas canister for the stove and lit a burner with a match to melt the lard. As the lard began to snap and crackle, he dropped hunks of dough into the fat.

The smell that wafted from the kitchen was to die for.

"Heavens!" Tessa gushed, unable to stop sniffing the air like a hungry wild animal. "That smells divine."

Dillon didn't turn around, but she saw the curl on his lips indicating he was awfully pleased with himself. While the biscuits were cooking, he pulled out slices of meat from the icebox and slipped them into the pan as well. The game meat began to fry with a smell similar to bacon, and he added more salt and spices. The scent was enough to make her drool.

Maybe his habit of providing isn't a bad thing after all, Tessa smirked, marveling at his cooking ability. She was about to get up and search the cupboards for plates and cups to set the table, when Dillon turned around.

"Stay right there," he ordered. "You've been through enough today, and I want you to relax."

He grabbed a plate and used a pair of tongs to lift the biscuits and meat from the pan, setting them on the china. Then he pulled a jar of honey from a cupboard and brought out two forks from a drawer. Heading over to the bed, he sat down next to her.

Tessa gazed at the piping hot meal. Given her level of hunger, it was a thing of pure beauty.

"Gosh, Dillon," she enthused, "a girl could really get used to this."

"That's the point," he said with a sparkle in his eye. "Now let's do something about those curves." He drizzled honey on a warm biscuit and lifted it to her lips.

"Mmmm," she took a bite and burst in rapture, "that's more like it!" She grabbed a fork and dug into hunks of meat and biscuit, stuffing them into her mouth. At this point, she didn't care if the meat was bison, venison, or squirrel, for that matter. The taste was out of this world. While she chewed, she closed her eyes and began to moan.

When she glanced at Dillon, her face flushed, realizing the sound she'd made was of unbridled ecstasy. He might be a bit miffed, she thought, compared to my response to his pemmican.

Dillon beat her to the save. "You're under no obligation to like everything I cook," he assured her. "As long as you keep making those sounds."

Tessa laughed, noticing his eyes were beaming. They both dove their forks into the meal, barely coming up for air. By the fourth bite, Tessa was beginning to feel human again. She twirled her fork happily as she chewed, observing how heavy it felt in her hand before she swallowed. Curious, she held up the fork to the lantern light, studying its prongs and the shape of the handle. Turning it over, she spied the .925 mark.

Solid silver.

Sterling, no less, with 92.5% silver content. It used to be her job to know such things on sight.

Tessa cast a glance at the other fork—it was identical. Most modern silverware was actually stainless steel, unless it happened to belong to an aristocratic family from a hundred years ago and was passed down as an heirloom.

"I found these here, when I first opened the cabin," Dillon noted, catching the way she marveled at the forks. He nodded at the plate they were using. "Along with some pieces of fine china, rimmed in gold. I guess the Bandits Hollow Gang lived the high life sometimes. My father used to tell me that my ancestor Iron Feather liked shiny things."

"Though he was Native American?"

"Because he was Native American. His people were from horse cultures that have a history of trading and raiding for supplies—whatever caught their eye. They loved their bling." He smiled a little. "Speaking of which," he set the empty plate down on the floor and held up the fork, running his finger down its elegant silver handle. "You promised."

Tessa's heart wobbled. She knew exactly what he was after. This morning, he'd dared to take her hunting for a glimpse into his world. Now it was *her* turn—

She toyed with her fork, nervous about exposing that part of herself to him—to *anyone*—when she spotted an odd etching on the fork handle that she hadn't noticed before. It was barely visible, on the same place where family initials are usually stamped onto heritage silverware.

It was a feather...

Just like the one she used to secretly mark on all her designs.

Tessa's heart began to skitter.

There was no way Dillon could know a feather was her secret symbol.

But perhaps Iron Feather did.

"Tessa," Dillon said softly, grasping the fork from her hand. "I want to see your passion now."

She nodded, trembling a little.

Then she stood to her feet, emotionally preparing herself to wedge that door open, gambling on the idea that maybe he truly did care about her. It was easier to keep that door shut, to protect herself from the inevitable crash and burn of relationships, as she'd learned so many times before. But the way Dillon gazed at her, with that intensity—and yearning—in his eyes, told her he was aching to peer inside. Drawing a deep breath, she secretly hoped that in doing so, she might finally be able to let a little bit of light into her heart.

For good.

19

Tessa sat at the table, gazing at the leather case she'd brought with her from New York. It had been in her backpack, luckily unharmed from the bear attack and after other wild animals had shredded her clothes in the middle of the night. So much for *ever* buying granola bars again, she thought. Unzipping the case to make it lie flat, she exposed the tools of her trade, scanning the gadgets held firm by little bands, all organized by function. There was a small anvil next to picks and hammers arranged by size, along with wire cutters, files, needle-nose pliers, solder, and chunks of sterling silver in a sack for melting. There was also a mold and material for sand casting, a crucible, and a hand-held torch.

She pulled out the mold and opened it up, grabbing a silver necklace she'd created at home in her spare time. She'd always wanted to make a feather pendant to go with it—something that would represent both her creativity and the strength to spread her wings, a symbol of rebellion from her "number" status at Jacquier & Co. It would be her own unique design, never worn by a celebrity anywhere.

Dillon sat down beside her, examining each of her tools as though they held clues to her soul. The ardent focus of his deep brown eyes made goosebumps course over her skin.

"I-I worked my way through art school, specializing in silver," she explained self-consciously, attempting to distract herself a little. "At my first job, I had free rein to create for the red-carpet set whatever kind of jewelry I wanted—as long as I agreed to be a number. To never put my name on any of my designs. I made good money, but it got pretty hollow, knowing there were people out there who would never have a clue who I really was." She turned to Dillon. "I bet you know the feeling from Vegas."

Dillon nodded, fascinated when she began to draw on the sand in the mold with a metal tool. With self-assured strokes, Tessa let her imagination roam free, creating a long, flowing feather, like the ones from Iron Feather that sat on Dillon's dresser. Her fingers worked to define a thin quill and delicate vanes. Dillon's eyes lit up at the spontaneity of her strokes, delighted at seeing her passion for artistry in action. He tilted his head, admiring the way her fingers made the feather curve and come alive in such a fragile, yet beautiful way, as if it might float upward at any moment from the sand. He watched while she dug a narrow funnel in the sand at the top of the mold so the silver could flow easily into the feather shape and fill in the area for the pendant.

"There," Tessa said, satisfied with the design. "You know, to save my sanity," she continued, feeling a nob swell in her throat at her confession, "I started secretly stamping this feather as my hallmark next to my employer's logo at my last job. It was my hidden calling card."

Her eyes sought Dillon's.

His gaze slid to the fork on the table with the feather etched into the handle, then over to his ancestor's owl feathers on the dresser, before his eyes returned to hers. He seemed intrigued, grasping the eerie coincidence. He reached up to brush a lock of hair from Tessa's forehead and gently swept it behind her ear, so it wouldn't fall near her design. His warm hand cupped her cheek.

He didn't say a word.

But Tessa felt the gravity of his gaze. She nodded, not quite understanding what it could all mean. Feathers, passion, a man she was falling for by the minute—one she'd only met a short time ago. Do things like this happen in real life? To a woman like her? All magical and feeling destined. And Lord have mercy—could it possibly last?

She turned shyly from Dillon, whose lips she had an urgent hankering to kiss, but she held herself back. She wanted to know if she could really trust him with her love of creativity— if he would maintain a sincere interest beyond the infatuation stage. Because to her, this wasn't a job. Her art was life—*her life* —the very reason she'd kept going despite difficult circumstances all this time. And it had to be treated with the same reverence Dillon had shown toward his mother's traditions.

Busying herself to avoid his stare, Tessa closed the sand mold and turned the clamp tight. She methodically took out chunks of silver from her sack and dropped them into a crucible, firing up her torch. Then she pointed the blue flame at the silver in a circular motion to melt the metal, adding a little flux to keep the fluidity. She artfully directed the flame to lick the silver chunks until they had become liquid. Satisfied, she poured the silver into the funnel of the sand mold to create her feather. Tessa got up to go to the kitchen and emptied some water from a jug into a small metal tray. When she returned to the table, she opened the sand cast and used tongs to lift the feather and dropped it into the water with a hiss. Sitting down beside Dillon, she removed the silver feather from the tray to show him.

His eyes roamed over the lovely creation she'd made, drawn by hand without any guidance whatsoever, now an actual silver feather before them. His appreciation for what she'd managed to do so easily, clearly after years of learning her craft, shone from his gaze.

Tessa was secretly thrilled.

"All I need is to solder a loop at the top of the feather for the necklace to hold," she explained, rather proud of herself. "Then I'll file off the edges and buff the pendant until it's smooth and shiny. After that, it will be ready to wear."

"Not yet," Dillon replied.

To her surprise, he slipped his arms around her waist and pulled her onto his lap, hugging her close. His chest felt hard, yet warm and inviting. She longed to allow her head to fall against his shoulder, letting her hair trickle down his back. But curiously, Dillon wriggled a hand into her front pocket. He pulled out the bandana he'd give her after the elk hunt—in all the ruckus, she'd forgotten it was there—and unwrapped it on the table. Inside the fabric were the two elk tusks, slightly brown at the edges from where the animal's blood had dried.

"These are your symbols of strength now." He gazed at the tusks. "You need to add one to your feather for balance."

Tessa was floored he was taking such an interest in the composition of her design, for what the pendant could represent.

Dillon wasn't finished yet. Her heart pounded when she saw him pull something else out of his pocket. A bear claw, also with dried blood clinging to the edges. She knew exactly where it came from—the bear who'd attacked her the other night. It was then she realized Dillon was hoping to participate in her design all along. He wanted to be part of her world—

Dillon set the claw on the table. It was huge, and the sight made the scratches on her back tingle again.

"I cut this from the bear that came after you," he admitted. "The one that's hanging in the barn. If you add these to your pendant—the tusk, the claw, the feather—it will bring a kind of harmony. Earth and air, fight and flight. The elements of your brave spirit."

A rush of raw sensation swirled inside Tessa. She hardly knew what to do with this feeling. Something about Dillon knew how to peer into her, how to cherish what he saw. She'd never felt so…understood.

And it made him as sexy as hell.

"Let me help," Dillon urged. "I want to feel what you feel."

His arms closed tighter. They felt warm and strong—like they were a part of her. Heart throbbing, she grasped one of the elk tusks and filed it down so none of the dried blood showed. She grabbed another file and fine grit sandpaper to make it look shiny. Then she wrapped the tusk in a thin bezel to test the size and turned on her torch, soldering the bezel to a silver plate. Trimming the edges with metal shears, she inserted the tusk back into the bezel and clamped it for a tight fit with needle-nose pliers, then filed the silver down so the tusk was perfectly set. Pulling out a piece of solder wire, she studied the feather, trying to figure out where to arrange the tusk.

Dillon startled her by pointing to the left of the feather quill. He gently grasped the elk tusk from her hand and placed it there. He took the bear claw and set it on the right.

"There, it's balanced now," he said with purpose in his tone, making her heart skip a beat.

"W-What do you mean?"

"Masculine and feminine. Like us. The claw and the tusk by the feather." His arms squeezed her. "They give power to each other. The way we do."

Tessa cheeks flushed with warmth.

He was right—

Something about Dillon's arrangement of the tusk and claw beside the feather gave the pendant a kind of grounding—along with a sense of magic. She couldn't help wondering if perhaps Dillon's mother used to have the same effect on him. More importantly, she realized no one had ever offered a suggestion for one of her designs she'd thought could actually work. That is, until Dillon. His artistic insight floored her.

Tessa clicked to ignite her torch and soldered the tusk next to the top of the quill. Then she gave Dillon a hand drill and pointed to where he could make a small hole in the bear claw that would accommodate a silver strand to connect it to the pendant necklace. Tessa used her torch to solder the claw, but when she clicked it off, she scratched her head, feeling like something was missing. Dillon reached into his pocket again.

He set down a piece of turquoise on the table.

To her astonishment, she recognized it from her mine. It was no longer raw, edged with pieces of host rock. The stone was shiny—and utterly beautiful. She gasped, turning to look at him.

"I scooped up a piece when we were in your mine," he admitted with mischief in his eyes. "You're not the only one who can polish things up. After an old farrier's rasp, some sandpaper and elbow grease did the trick. Here, try putting it at the top of the feather quill. My mother would say the turquoise represents sky, what the Zuni call Skystone."

Tessa gave it a shot, admiring his taste. To her, the pendant looked perfect now, evenly balanced between earth and air. She loved it.

"Hey, you're good at this!" she marveled. "We make a great team. Especially with your mother's, well, influence. By the way, you haven't told me much about her."

While Tessa set a bezel around the lovely turquoise and soldered it to a plate, Dillon watched her intently.

"Well, like I mentioned, she was Apache. Jicarilla, the same as Iron Feather's people," he said. "She grew up in the mountains learning the old ways. Like my ancestor, she learned to straddle two worlds."

"Two worlds?"

"The old ways—and the white man's world."

"You said Iron Feather was Ute, too."

"Like my dad," Dillon nodded. "They often intermarried back in those days. But my father was blonde—white enough to pass, as they say. My mother really loved him, so she left the reservation. Whenever the three of us brothers were with our mom as kids, people assumed Lander was adopted. It scarred him when we got to reform school. They laughed at his light hair and accused him of being from my mother's lover. Barrett has dark hair like my mom, but he cuts it short."

"We met, remember?" She arched a brow. "I sat bound and gagged in the back of his cruiser. Thank God he untied me before we got to the hotel."

Tessa could feel Dillon chuckle beneath her legs. As she continued to file the spare silver from around the turquoise and placed it at the top of the feather quill, he nuzzled his chin against the curve of her neck.

"I bet you miss your parents," she said softly.

"I bet you do, too," he whispered against her skin. "They must no longer be around—you don't talk about them."

Tessa nodded. Intuitively, she knew they were getting to the heart of things now. To the kind of pain that had perhaps kept her and Dillon back in life, and maybe in relationships, without realizing it.

"My parents were divorced when I was really young, and my mom passed away before I went to art school. So I guess I'm in the same boat as you. We've always been on our own, huh? Maybe that's forced us to be a bit over protective about our hearts…"

Tessa voice trailed off as she studied the intense blues and greens in the turquoise, no longer dulled by the crustiness of the host rock. A part of her longed for her heart to be just as vibrant, not dragged down by the pain of past disappointments. She stroked the stone with her finger, enjoying the feel of its smooth surface. "I'm curious," she asked, "what made you pocket a piece of my turquoise, then polish it? Does this kind of stone mean something special to you?"

Dillon remained silent for a while, as though cautious about sharing such information. He watched while Tessa clicked on her torch and soldered the stone to the top of the pendant, attaching a ring for the necklace to go through. When she was done, he reached out his hand to stroke the colorful stone.

"*Dáatł'iiji* provides protection for my mother's people," he noted. "For generations, women tied it to cradle boards to prevent witchcraft from harming their children. It also helps a warrior's aim. I used to carry the stone my ancestor handed down in my waistband whenever I entered a match in Las Vegas. I never lost a fight. But the thing is—"

He paused for a moment. She could tell he was weighing whether to say something. After a time, she felt his chest expand with an intake of breath. The exhale that followed seemed to come as a kind of release.

"My mother could hear the stones," he stated carefully. "She said they sang to her. It was one of the gifts she received after her Apache coming-of-age ceremony. Even to this day, teenagers are encouraged to have visions and find their gifts."

Tessa stared for a spell into the colors of the stone, so alive that it wasn't hard for her to imagine hearing them speak. Boldly, she turned around in Dillon's lap to face him.

"What happened?" she said. "In reform school. I mean, that made you so angry? That turned you into that dangerous guy I first saw when you came out with your shotgun on your porch. Didn't your ancestor's turquoise protect you back then?"

Dillon's jaw began to twist, the muscles rippling over his hard cheeks. He looked down so she wouldn't see the rage that flared, but it didn't work. Stubbornly, she lifted up his chin with her fingers. She dared to stare directly into his eyes. Into his angry heart.

"I didn't...want it to," he replied slowly.

Tessa searched his face, puzzled.

"Because?" She paused, attempting to sort through his words, to make sense of his odd confession. "You wanted...to show them...how tough you were?"

Dillon's eyes didn't flinch. She knew she'd nailed it. But there was something that had been bugging her for days. Swallowing hard, she worked up the nerve to ask him.

"Dillon, what does Big *Yi'yee* mean?"

A tremor sped through his entire body.

Tessa realized then that she'd touched a nerve. She'd never seen him thrown off guard before. He always seemed direct, sure. Now she saw in his eyes that he was actually rattled. Tilting her head, she drew a deep breath.

"It's time for the truth, Dillon. We can't ever be really... together. If we're a threesome, I mean."

He searched her eyes, confused.

"If Big *Yi'yee* comes between us."

She grasped his cheek gently with her hand, allowing her warmth to seep into his skin.

"He's still here, right now, isn't he? Filling up the room. Iron Feather told me, when I saw him at the creek. He said he's the one who makes you cold sometimes. Who is he, Dillon?"

He glanced at the two owl feathers on his dresser, next to his ancestor's old, suede medicine bag, filled with secrets. When his eyes locked again on Tessa's, he appeared caught in a snare.

And she wasn't having any of it. Her eyes drilled into his with the same intensity he'd often showed to her.

"Dillon, you said you wanted me. That you care about me. And even though it's fast, it's very real for you. Well so is this—"

She brushed back her hair, allowing her gaze to fix on his again, searing in focus. "And there's something I want you to know. I'm not about to share you with any of your past shadows. Whatever this thing is that makes you go cold sometimes, it's got to leave the room for good—and our lives."

Dillon's eyes drifted to the floor, studying the grain of wood. His gaze returned to Tessa.

"My people have a story from long ago," he began. "Of Big *Yi'yee* who devours men. He's a legendary owl."

Tessa shivered. "I-I don't understand. When I saw Iron Feather...I know this sounds crazy...but he became—"

"An owl."

It wasn't a question, but a fact from Dillon.

"What's that all about?" she implored. "Was I delirious from falling in the stream? From hypothermia?"

He became quiet. He shifted his stare to the wood stove on the other side of the room, watching the leap of flames. Then he picked up the pendant on the table, holding it at the bottom of the feather with the piece of turquoise closest to Tessa.

"Touch it," he said. He stared at the blue-green colors that glistened in the fire light.

"It's cold," she replied.

Dillon glanced in her eyes. "I used the power of the turquoise not for protection, but for better aim. To kill—"

Tessa wrestled inside with that information. His confession unnerved her, mainly because it didn't seem to scare him at all. It came so naturally.

"In our tradition, Big *Yi'yee* learned he can devour men, or help them. Cold or warm."

"And you used it only for…cold. Didn't you? Then why did Iron Feather turn before me into an owl?"

"Because he'd decided to use his powers for good. That's why he became a medicine man. For the Apache, the Ute, any of the tribes in the late nineteenth century who needed him."

"How?"

"The children," Dillon said. "It was always about the children. Iron Feather was more than a famous outlaw. This was the era when children were being ripped from their tribes and sent to boarding schools, sometimes as far away as Pennsylvania. They were forced to give up their traditions and languages—their whole identities—without seeing their parents for years. Iron Feather took them back."

"Back? Y-You mean he kidnapped them or something?"

"I told you all along he was a renowned tracker. He used the money he got to find the children and bring them home, back to their tribes. The government never caught him—he was as slippery as hell."

"Are you saying…he robbed trains to finance his way to return the children?"

Dillon nodded.

"Then you can overcome the coldness, too. Iron Feather told me something out there—it was the key. He said you need to listen to the stones. Like your mother. Before he turned back into an owl and flew away."

Tessa grasped the pendant from his hand and held it up, admiring what they'd created together. She swiveled to the table and grabbed the silver necklace she'd made, looping it through the ring she'd put at the top of the turquoise stone. The jewelry looked brilliant in the firelight—the tusk, the claw, and the turquoise a perfect balance with the silver feather. "Take off your shirt," she insisted.

He slipped off his camo shirt. She could see his heart pounding against his chest. His eyes checked hers.

Tessa gently placed the necklace over his head, letting the pendant fall against his tan skin. Leaning toward him, she kissed the stone, then his hard chest. She lifted her lips to his.

"It's time to make the turquoise warm, Dillon. Along with your heart."

She roamed her hands along his broad, muscled shoulders, relishing the feel of his hard body, then slipped her fingers down to his waist. Grasping the bottom of her shirt, she pulled it over her shoulders and let it drop to the floor. Unclasping her bra, she allowed her lavish breasts to spill against him, pressing the warmth of her skin to his.

"It's time."

20

Dillon lifted Tessa in his strong arms and gazed into her eyes, watching the firelight dance in their luminous blue-green. He stepped over to the bed and gently set her down. For a long while, he simply beheld her face, his eyes tracing her blonde hair that flowed over her pale shoulders to the pillow.

"My God, you're beautiful," he whispered.

He reached down to tenderly unzip her pants, and she let him, watching him remove them to take in the length of her legs and delicate feet. His gaze followed to her ample hips and small waist, rising to her breasts. His eyes met hers.

Dillon's longing was so fierce it filled the air, making the molecules around them feel as thick as steam.

He shed his pants to the floor, and Tessa was in awe of his sculpted physique again—something she could never quite get over. The only adornment on his body was the pendant they'd made, shining like his eyes in the flickering light. His long hair fell past his broad shoulders and chest.

Her eyes were riveted to him—

Dillon was breathtaking.

Gently, he laid down beside her. He appeared hesitant to brush against her skin that would surely release a powerful need in him, verging on brutal. The very proximity of her soft, elegant body made Dillon's jaw clench in restraint. She grabbed his face anyway and pulled him to her for a kiss. Not just any kiss—she linked her leg over his hard hips and pressed her breasts to his chest, devouring him. Dillon's arms wrapped around Tessa and her breasts felt pillowy against his skin as he crushed her tighter. His hand searched for the curve of her hip, relishing the smoothness of her extraordinary skin.

Tessa was all woman—delicate yet full at the same time—like no one he'd ever witnessed among the gym bunnies at training centers, who constantly tried to force their bodies into hard, sinewy angles with fake breasts attached. Nothing was fake about Tessa. Her body was *real* with a lushness that could never be imitated by plastic surgery. Every curve was so sensual it practically made his body scream, wanting to fill himself up with the refined roundness of her like a rare delicacy.

Dillon's hands roamed all over Tessa, reveling in her—the tiny waist and swollen hips and breasts, with skin the color of warm pearl by the light of the fire. His need raged within, and he couldn't stop himself from rolling on top of her, bowing his head to lick her breasts. Tessa arched her back and released a moan, her legs writhing slightly at the feel of his warm lips on her nipples. The pendant around his neck dropped to rest on her cleavage as his tongue circled, moving from one breast to the other. His hard chest expanded as though her body swelled him with life. She reached up to touch the turquoise stone that rested against her skin.

"It's warmer now," she teased.

"That's not the only thing that's going to get hot."

His eyes glinted as he ran his finger along her cleavage down her waist, circling her navel and gently using his knee to open her hips. He descended upon the cleft between her thighs, artfully swirling his tongue until she thought she would burst into fire. His long hair draped over her legs, and Tessa grabbed fiercely at him, unable to stop herself from pulling him deeper. Again, her back arched and her legs began to twist while her lips exhaled the sound of ecstasy he loved. Dillon brushed his erection against her skin to tease her, sliding it over her slick folds. Tessa opened her eyes, taking in the raw gorgeousness of this man, every muscle in his body flexed tight. She reached up and pulled his face to hers for another kiss, and he fell against her, whipping her body around so that she was on top him. His long, hardness demanded her, and she smiled, leaning down to place her lips on the tip. She caressed with her tongue, licking and sucking, the way she'd been secretly dying to do for days. She wanted to consume Dillon, to merge their bodies with a force that might never separate. Her blonde hair tousled against his hips as she licked him up and down, watching him close his eyes and groan.

"Tessa, not yet," he insisted, pulling her up with his powerful arms to press her breasts against his chest. Greedily, his hands swam over her skin, wanting to touch and stroke every inch of her. He reached down beside the bed and grabbed a condom he'd left there, ripping it open and applying it over his firm flesh. Then he deftly ran his hand between her legs along her velvety folds, pulsing against the warm wetness that made him smile. To Tessa's surprise, he took off the necklace and set it between her breasts, which were so plump they easily kept the pendant firm.

With a sharp gasp she felt him slip inside her, hard and slick, and their skin seemed to meld into their heat like one being. With near-violent force, Dillon grabbed her hips and crashed her to him. But then he moved inside her with long, slow thrusts. He watched her eyes, reveling in her excitement. Tessa moaned with a deep rumble from her chest that ended in a soft wail, almost like a purr. Swaying against one another, they drove each other to a rhythmic, blistering edge. Dillon dove into her breasts again, sipping and sucking, his face filled with her roundness. When he extended his arm to pulse his fingers against her wet folds, circling with skillful pressure, she felt lightning begin to rip through her, bursting inside with hot sparks.

"Dillon!" she cried, thrusting her hips. "Now—"

He clutched the small of her back and tumbled her body beneath him again. Once on top, he unleashed his full power. He pumped with an animal ferocity that left her reeling. Tessa thrust her arms wide across the bed, surrendering to his driving force. Wave upon wave of more ecstasy rippled through her, the fire between her legs hot and making her cry out, wondering if it was possible to pass out from pleasure.

What a way to die, she thought.

Yet Dillon wouldn't stop—

She clutched the linens in another burst of excitement and screamed, his hard thrusts pushing her to insanity.

"Come with me, Dillon!" She grabbed at his back.

"Oh, Tessa—"

He buried his final thrust into her, every muscle in his body flexed as she dug her fingers into his skin. Suddenly, all Tessa could see was white. Dillon cried out and collapsed against her, pressed upon her breasts as sweat rippled between their skin.

Heaving ragged breaths, they held onto each other with a grip that made letting go seem impossible. Dillon's long hair laced over Tessa's shoulders, and she reached up to stroke his cheek, her body beaded in sweat. He picked up the pendant at her cleavage and smoothed away the glossy moisture. Gazing at the turquoise, he checked Tessa's eyes, admiring the match of color. Then he threaded his fingers through her hair before he buried his lips in hers for another kiss.

"Male and female, earth and sky," he whispered.

For a long time, he simply stared at her face once again, studying each of her features—her eyes, nose, cheeks and lips—as though they were jewels.

"It's you, Tessa."

He brought the turquoise from the pendant to her cheek and pressed it so she could feel its warmth.

"You're the balance. You're the heat."

21

After a few minutes, Tessa wriggled from underneath Dillon with a mischievous look in her eye. Slipping the necklace around her neck again, she got up from the bed and headed to the kitchen, feeling his intense gaze admire the sway of her hips and the way firelight fell across her body. She pulled two crystal glasses from a cupboard, rimmed in gold like his other antique china. Then she grabbed the bottle of Cuervo by the stove along with a knife that hung in the kitchen. Stepping toward him, her natural breasts bounced with her gait and her lips curled into a sly smile. She sat down beside Dillon on the bed and placed the glasses and tequila on the floor. For a moment, she stared at the torn, faded label with Spanish words on the bottle and the image of a black crow on its cork.

"Bet you found this too, when you first opened the cabin," she remarked, intrigued by the golden color of the liquor. "With its age, do you think it's any good?"

Dillon nodded, breaking into a smile when she picked up the bottle and brazenly broke the seal and pulled off the cork, which was so old it nearly crumbled in her hand. He clearly enjoyed seeing her naked, and her curves sent glints of admiration to his eyes while she poured them each a shot in the glasses and held one to him. He sat up on the bed with her and grasped the glass, curiosity in his gaze when she lifted the knife.

"You made a deal, Dillon," she said, tracing a crisscross motion against her palm. She picked up the pendant between her breasts. "You saw something today I never show anyone—how I make my designs. So maybe we sealed our, um… physical connection…just now," she smirked, running a finger teasingly down his firm chest. "But I want your oath never to speak of my creative process to anybody. And I won't breathe a word of your mother's traditions. Ready?"

Dillon took the knife from her. "Only if you make me a promise," he said in a serious tone.

She regarded his brown eyes, detecting that what he was about to say mattered enormously to him. She gave him a nod.

"Stay."

He carved an X into his flesh without so much as a wince. The blood pooled on his hand and dripped onto the sheets, but he didn't care. He held up his palm like an offering.

"Please stay, Tessa. I'll do everything in my power to keep Big *Yi'yee* at bay. As long as you help keep my heart warm."

Tessa's eyes widened at the blood that trickled down his wrist, noticing his gaze never left hers for a second.

This was serious—

She understood if she cut her hand in return, it was about

more than an oath. It was about *them*, being together, relying on each other to forge a way forward while casting away shadows.

"Then you'd better keep your promise, Dillon Iron Feather," she warned. "If you want me to stay, your heart has to remain as warm as the sun and beating free. Nothing between us anymore. Agreed?"

Dillon nodded slowly, and Tessa bravely held out her hand, sucking in a breath. With amazing swiftness, he sliced her skin faster than she could feel it, barely registering a sting. They clasped palms and held their glasses for a toast.

"To sacred secrets," Dillon said.

With a clink, they downed their shots of tequila and gasped, coming up for air. The alcohol was powerful, concentrated by over a century in the bottle, yet tasted of mellow oak and agave mixed with something warm and magical, as though it had been suffused by rays of sunlight.

Dillon stared at the bottle of Cuervo, focused on the vintage label. A tenderness seeped into his eyes that yanked at Tessa's heart. He held the bottle to her. "May what we have last just as long," he said, leaning in for a kiss.

"Tessa," he whispered, breaking away to study her face. For a moment, his big brown eyes searched hers. "I do believe they call this…love."

"Is that right?" she teased, swiping another kiss. Nevertheless, her breath hitched, her heart skittering out of control that he'd dared to mention that word. The L word…

Dillon didn't take in the lightness of her bait for a second. He stared at her intently, making a tremor slip its way along the back of her neck. In silence, he squeezed his hand tighter over their crisscross wounds.

"That's exactly right." His grip was so strong it nearly hurt, but he wouldn't let go. "And as you've probably figured out by now," he added. "I'm a man of my word."

In the following two weeks, Tessa and Dillon carefully carved out more turquoise from the vein in her mine. Then they made jewelry together—rings, bracelets, cuffs. Each time, Dillon was fascinated by her silversmith skills and creativity. The most important thing to Tessa, however, was that she make a pendant for Nell like the one she'd designed for herself. She'd promised to report how she was doing, and she wanted to thank her for her support with a piece of jewelry containing a stone from her own mine. Dillon helped with the creation until they were both proud of the gift that featured the other elk tusk and a bear claw along with a silver feather. On a Friday morning at sunrise, they headed to Bandits Hollow to present it to Nell at an early hour, when the hotel and restaurant tended to be slow.

But Dillon had an ulterior motive for the trip, which he freely admitted to Tessa. He knew Barrett liked to get Nell's breakfast special, and he wanted to catch up with him before his shift so he could find out what was going on with Bill Crouch and his illegal mining.

When Dillon and Tessa arrived in Bandits Hollow, like clockwork, there was Barrett's cruiser parked outside the restaurant. They spied him through the window wolfing down a platter of ham, scrambled eggs and hash browns. Barrett glanced up and caught his brother and Tessa walking toward the door. He acknowledged them with a tip of his hat.

The minute Nell saw the two of them swing open the door of the lobby, she clasped her hands, her mouth stretching into a smile. "Good morning! Ain't you two a sight." Stepping around the front desk to greet them, she hugged Tessa. "How's my brave young miner?" Nell lifted her chin and regarded Dillon with a discerning eye. "Is this bad boy getting in your way? You say the word and I'll slap him back into line—"

"No!" Tessa grinned. "As a matter of fact, he's actually been helping me. I may not have found gold yet, but I did discover this."

She reached into her pocket and pressed a polished stone into Nell's palm.

"It's high-grade turquoise, with a really rich color that I can put into my designs. I'm beyond thrilled, and you're the one who gave me the courage to keep pursuing it." Tessa's eyes became misty at the edges. "I'll never forget that."

She gripped Nell for another hug, a bit surprised when she let her go that Nell was blinking back tears, too. It clearly meant a lot to her to see another local woman succeed. Tessa squeezed her arm. "Will you be around for a while? We wanted to chat with Barrett for a minute. Then I have something for you."

"Sure," Nell nodded with a smile. "I'll be right here, business as usual."

Tessa followed after Dillon into the restaurant to join Barrett. They slid into the cowhide seat across from him in a booth, watching him go at his breakfast like he was trying to break a land record. When he finished chewing a large mouthful, he washed it down with a gulp of coffee.

"Yo, bro. What's up?" he said.

Dillon grabbed a fork on top of a folded, red-bandana napkin and boldly dug into his brother's eggs.

"Breakfast, for starters," he smirked. "On you, of course—"

"Aw, come on," Barrett protested. "You never come see me unless you want something. Start talking."

Lila stopped by their booth and turned over two mugs, filling them with coffee before Dillon and Tessa had a chance to ask. "Nice to see you again, honey!" she said brightly, her gaze dipping to Tessa's leg beneath the table, where Dillon's hand rested on her knee. She gave Tessa a wink. "Looks like you ain't got man trouble no more."

Tessa blushed. "Well, maybe it's all that fresh air around here," she conceded.

"Then breathe in deep, girl!" Lila replied, sashaying her hips as she walked away to another booth across the room.

Barrett couldn't help eyeing the sassy swing of her step, till Dillon shook his arm.

"Placer mining," he reminded him. "On BLM land. Near Lander's spread that we saw a while back. Did you check it out? What's going on—"

"Whole lot of nothing." Barrett heaved a sigh. "It's damn hard to get up there. You oughta know, from all the hunting you do. I rounded up a couple officers, and we couldn't make it to the site with ATVs, so we had to saddle horses to check it out. By the time we arrived, there was nothing."

"What do you mean, nothing?" Dillon pressed.

"Just like it sounds—whoever was responsible had removed all the machinery. They probably discovered your tracks and figured someone had been watching. They even graded the ground to make it look like construction vehicles had never been there. But you can't ignore the tailings of river rock. The piles had been spread to make it look natural, but there was too much stone on the banks for an ordinary river. Something clearly happened, so I took pictures and questioned Bill Crouch. He denied it, of course. Without better evidence of who was involved, I got nothing to work with."

Barrett clashed his fork against Dillon's to shove it from his plate like a sibling accustomed to competing for food. He stabbed a hunk of country ham and stuffed it in his mouth.

"You mentioned you thought you recognized some of Crouch's ranch hands doing the dirty work," Barrett continued, chewing. "You figure he's left that spot to find another lode near the new mine about a mile from your place? Word on the street says the vein stretches all the way from a divide by your cabin to the BLM location near Lander. If Crouch is after a secret route to that vein, then there's another chance I can catch him."

Dillon glanced at Tessa. "All I know is that Crouch trespassed into Tessa's mine earlier this month. I think he's gotten a hold of geological maps for the area, and he's determined to siphon off this vein wherever he can—on the surface or deeper in the ground. He's got gold fever, and I wouldn't put anything past him."

"Then you'd better be careful," Barrett lowered his brows. "Because a man like that isn't going to stop because somebody thwarted him once. He's ruthless. I'll tell the other officers to keep an eye out and question him again."

Barrett nabbed one more bite of hash browns before he got up. He gave Tessa a cautious smile. "Nice to see you again, ma'am." He put five bucks on the table and left the rest of his breakfast for Dillon, then tipped his hat. "I gotta run."

She watched Barrett stride out of the restaurant before she turned to Dillon. "Do you think Crouch might show up at my mine again?"

He forked hash browns from Barrett's plate and chewed slowly. "That would be mighty risky," he said, "since he knows by now somebody's watching him. Even so, you'd be amazed at what gold fever can make a man do." Shaking his head, he pushed aside the plate. "How about we give Nell your gift now, while we're here?"

Tessa nodded, her stomach fluttering with butterflies, hoping Nell would like it. As they got up, Dillon placed a twenty-dollar bill on the table and they headed to the lobby. With each step, Tessa drew nervous breaths of anticipation.

"Hey Nell," she called out softly. "Do you, um, have a minute?"

Nell tilted her head. "Of course," she replied cheerfully. "What's on your mind? You got enough supplies out there? You know, you can always come back here for a good meal and sneak in a bonafide shower. Heaven knows, Dillon's place doesn't exactly provide the high life."

Tessa laughed. "Well, the creek *is* awfully cold. But I've gotten used to heating up the water."

"Hmm," she eyed the way Tessa and Dillon stood close to

each other, chuckling a little. "Seems to me you've gotten used to heating up other things, too."

Tessa's cheeks rifled with warmth. She dropped her gaze while digging into her pocket. "Here, I wanted to give you this," she pulled out the necklace with the pendant and held it up, eager to change the subject. "This is for you. Dillon and I designed it. It's to thank you, you know, for everything—"

"Oh my stars!" Nell gasped, wide eyed. "That's the single, most beautiful thing I've ever seen! My God, Tessa, you sure?"

"Of course!" she replied. "I told you I'm a jeweler—"

"But honey, I had no idea! This looks like something rich ladies from Dallas wear, when they blow through here on their way to Aspen. So the turquoise and other pieces are from Colorado?" Nell searched Tessa's eyes. "Are you intending to sell these designs?"

"Absolutely," Tessa replied. "That's been my game plan all along, why I made the leap from New York to Colorado. You really like it?"

"Like it?" To Tessa's astonishment, Nell placed the necklace across the lobby desk and pulled out her cell phone to snap a picture. "Sweetie, how much do you charge for this? It's extraordinary! People would pay thousands for it in places like Aspen or Telluride. Here, I'll prove it to you. I've known Betty for ages, and she owns one of the most exclusive shops in Colorado—"

Before Tessa realized what she was doing, Nell pressed a contact on her phone and forwarded the picture of the necklace. Within seconds, her cell was ringing.

"Bet that woke you up, didn't it?" Nell answered, grinning. "Just thought I'd add a little sparkle to your morning, Betty."

Tessa and Dillon could hear the woman jabbering excitedly on the other end, but they couldn't make out her words.

"Oh, it's just a little bauble created by a friend of mine." Nell winked. "Handmade with genuine silver and all-natural elements from Colorado. Think your customers might be interested?"

Nell held up her phone, pressing the speaker function to unleash a torrent of enthusiasm from her friend.

"That necklace is the most stunning thing I've ever seen!" Betty cried. "*Of course* my customers will want it! Does your friend do custom orders? When can he or she come to my shop?"

"They'll be there in a week!" Nell grinned. "Just in time for the Spirit Festival. You always get a flood of tourists and need more inventory then, right? Count on that Saturday, bright and early. Thanks, honey!"

Nell clicked off her phone, beaming.

"Better get busy," she urged Tessa. She smiled while she slipped the necklace over her head, admiring the way the silver pendant shone against the maroon of her rodeo shirt. "Because you're about to launch your business at *Midnight Serenade*. The highest-end shop in Telluride."

22

By the time they drove to Telluride for the Spirit Festival, Tessa couldn't decide if her frayed nerves meant she was excited or exhausted. She and Dillon had been working on more designs non-stop, and she deeply appreciated his artistic instincts that helped balance out her creations. With each piece of jewelry they finished, she stamped the back with her hallmark feather and etched her name in bold letters:

Tessa Grove Designs.

It felt wonderful to finally see her dream coming true.

And to share it with a man she was falling in love with more and more every step of the way.

She'd asked Dillon while they were working if he wanted credit for the designs too, since he freely added ideas that blended more elements of earth: antler prong tips, claws, petrified wood, even fossils they'd found on the ground from when Colorado was covered by an ancient sea. Dillon merely smiled and shook his head.

"I've tasted enough fame for one lifetime," he replied. "And in case nobody ever told you," he slipped his thick arms around her at the cabin table where they were working, "men who are comfortable in their own skin aren't afraid to let women shine."

Tessa felt a warmth bloom in her heart, but a hesitation, too.

"Are you comfortable in your skin now, Dillon?"

He snuggled his chin against her neck, enjoying the heat of her body. Gently, he turned his face to absorb her in a kiss. Then he brushed back strands of her hair and grasped her temples.

"I think the real question is, are *you*?"

Tessa searched his eyes, not quite grasping his intention.

His face became stone again, and she found his gaze difficult to endure. His large brown eyes seemed to collect shadows at the edges, which he deliberately willed away.

"Tessa," he bowed his forehead to hers. "I know what it's like to be beaten down. To have people dismiss you. Or worse, laugh and tear you apart, simply because they think they're more powerful. It happened at reform school and later in my fighting career. You're about to enter the big time. And if there's anything I've learned, it's this: You've got to own it."

He reached to the table and picked up the latest pendant she'd made: a lovely silver leaf bordered by turquoise and a curved tip of antler. He turned it over and examined her signature on the back.

"It's time to really *be* Tessa Grove. Beautiful. Powerful. And brilliant."

He swept back her hair for another kiss.

"Be completely comfortable with who you are. Your talent, knowing there's no one else quite like you. If you don't walk into Betty's shop fully ready to sell that, everyone's going to feel it. They'll make mince meat out of you, one way or another. Like my mother always said about hunting: patience and precision. This is your shot, Tessa. Make it yours."

During the long drive, Tessa kept repeating Dillon's words over and over to herself like a mantra. As they finally entered the town of Telluride, they turned down Colorado Avenue, the main thoroughfare of the historic village nestled in a box canyon against the stunning backdrop of the San Juan Mountains. She couldn't help rubbernecking at the charming shops and boutiques that lined the picturesque street, which appeared quaint and welcoming.

But Tessa wasn't fooled—she knew that despite the low-key atmosphere, many of the richest people in the world had homes here. Ralph Lauren, Oprah Winfrey, and a host of tycoons who didn't care for the paparazzi glitz of places like Park City or Aspen. Even her former boss at Jacquier & Co. used to moan that he'd never succeeded in selling to shops in Telluride—and with his pushiness and love of garish bling, it was easy to see why. People here wore casual jeans and hiking boots, and there wasn't a Gucci or Versace storefront in sight.

But that didn't mean they didn't have gold bricks in their pockets.

Dillon steered his truck to the *Midnight Serenade* boutique, and Tessa felt her pulse quicken. She studied the jewelry on the blue velvet display in the front window, set off by delicate gold stars that hung from the ceiling, admiring the world-class quality of the gems. Opening the truck door, she hauled in a breath.

"Time to step into the spotlight," she smiled at Dillon, straightening her back and putting on her best game face, the way he'd taught her. "I am the real deal," she whispered. "And Betty is going to fall in love with my designs."

She grabbed the vintage traveling case they'd found in a closet in Dillon's cabin and stepped out of the truck, pausing to take in the moment. Every piece of jewelry she'd created was lovingly arranged inside the case for display, fasted by thin leather strips, so she gripped the handle with confidence and wore a smile.

No sooner did she take big strides toward the shop, when a skinny, middle-aged man in a suit burst through the door onto the sidewalk. In his hurry, he slammed right into Tessa and toppled them both to ground, sending her case and jewelry flying. Ignoring her, he cursed at the pavement and threw a crumpled business card to the ground.

Dillon rushed to her side. He swiftly lifted Tessa to her feet and braced her shoulders. Despite his support, her mouth flung open in shock.

"M-My old boss," she stuttered, hardly loud enough for Dillon to hear. "The one who called me a number—"

In a split-second, Arthur Jacquier scrambled to his feet,

startled when he recognized Tessa. He spotted her case that had fallen open, eyeing her jewelry. Glancing up, he crossed his arms and broke into a grin.

"Tessa!" he scolded as if she were a disobedient pet. "Don't tell me you've become a carpetbagger!" He rocked back on his heels and laughed. "I can't believe you'd try to sell your cheap knock-offs in Telluride. You know, all I have to do is rub elbows with the right retailers and inform them you're using fake stones to copy my brand."

Dillon fetched the crumpled business card he'd thrown on the ground and unfolded it. "Like the owner of *Midnight Serenade*?" He held it up. "Looks more like you're rubbing elbows with the sidewalk. She threw you out, didn't she?"

"Who is this Cro-Magnon?" Arthur fumed. He brushed off his designer suit, pressing the fabric flat. Then his lips curled into an odd, knowing smirk that made Tessa shudder. The reptilian look in his eyes reminded her of Bill Crouch when he'd come to her mine, wearing that strangely jolly expression to hide his ruthlessness.

"I've a mind to warn Betty who you really are. Another ungrateful artist trying to dupe retailers—"

Arthur's words caught in his throat as his feet began to rise in air. Wild eyed, his scrawny legs squirmed while Dillon held him firm at eye level with his thick fists at his lapels.

"You're going to do *what?*" Dillon said in a deep growl. He turned and slammed Arthur against the side of the shop, his eyes burning fire.

Arthur's face sank in terror. A trickle of liquid sped down his pants leg and stained the sidewalk.

"Dillon!" Tessa warned, recalling that his last opponent

ended up in a coma. She jiggled his arm. "Stop! He's not worth it. We're here for my jewelry today. This is my big break—"

As though a spell had been broken, Dillon shook his head, allowing his grip to loosen. He opened his fingers and stepped back, letting Arthur drop to the ground.

"You're the luckiest bastard on earth," he hissed, glaring at him. "If we didn't have something better to do right now, your face would be inseparable from the pavement."

A limousine rolled up on the street and gave a light honk. The driver got out and trotted to the passenger door, swinging it open and nodding at Arthur. Gathering his feet beneath him, Arthur bolted for the vehicle.

"Which shop to next, Mister Jacquier?" asked the driver before he shut the door.

"Just get me the hell out of here!" Arthur barked, rolling up his tinted window to make himself disappear.

As the limousine sped off, Tessa dove for a couple of pieces of jewelry that had fallen out on the sidewalk, placing them carefully back into her case. She snapped it closed and tucked it under her arm, trembling.

"What's wrong?" said Dillon, peering into her eyes.

"H-He's more powerful than you realize," she said on the verge of tears. "He has dozens of clients who walk the red carpet. They're A-listers in music and film. Didn't you hear what he said? He's going to run around claiming my stones are fake. He'll ruin my reputation before I even get started—"

Without warning, Dillon grabbed her shoulders and swiveled her to face the front window of *Midnight Serenade*.

"Do you really think the same woman who displays jewels

like that is going to be fooled?" He shook her shoulders a little. "Real knows real, Tessa. Try pawning a fake stone or copy on you—much less on Betty. This isn't about what Arthur said."

"What do you mean?" she stiffened.

"This is about your fear. And it's a lie."

Before she knew it, Dillon had pulled her to the side of the building where no one could see them. His eyes studied hers.

"You're a mountain, Tessa. That's why I kept adding elements of earth to your designs. Because from the first moment I saw you, I knew your spirit was strong. And it was no surprise you discovered turquoise."

"What?" she said. "But the claim was for a gold mine—"

Dillon nodded, holding up his hand.

"When I was a boy, my mom used to call a mountain near our home *Djit Dáatł'iji*. Turquoise Mountain, for the way it looked at twilight, tinted blue with the sun behind it. She told me an old Apache tale of a girl who dug a hole in the ground and turned into a bear. Though she was young, she acquired the bear's strength. Her ferocity pushed people to reach for the stars to become the Pleiades. One day, my mother said I'd find a woman that strong. She'd be mighty as the bear inside, her eyes as beautiful as turquoise, who reaches for the stars."

A tear snuck down Tessa's cheek. She bit her lip, holding her breath.

"My mother listened to the stones," Dillon reminded her, brushing the moisture from her cheek. "And she told me I would know who was the one. From the day I met you, I knew it was you."

Tessa hugged him tightly, pressing her head into his shoulder.

"I don't feel strong right now. You saw how Arthur had me totally derailed. His connections could destroy me—"

"The bear came into your life for a reason. It's time to go after what you want, and rely on your strength. It doesn't matter what Arthur says. The only thing that matters right now is what *you* say. To Betty."

Dillon took her by the hand and led her to the door of the shop. He squeezed her fingers. "Be brave enough to size up your opponent and surprise the hell out of him. What's the one thing Arthur never thought you'd do?"

Tessa stared at the door as if it were a portal to a whole new world.

"Be successful, on my own. With no influence or help from him."

Dillon kissed her on the cheek and smiled.

"Then go for it, city girl."

23

"Oh my Lord," Betty's mouth dropped when she turned over one of Tessa's silver pendants. "It's got the feather—"

She swiftly flipped over all the jewelry on top of her glass display case that Tessa had set out for her, making loud clinks. "I had no idea." She ran her hands through her black, bobbed hair. "Nell didn't tell me."

Tessa's cheeks began to burn.

She thought for certain Arthur had somehow already contacted Betty and tarnished her reputation. For all she knew, he'd called his lawyer to start a case on copyright infringement of Jacquier & Co.'s designs. "The turquoise is *real*," she defended adamantly. "I never use fake stones, honest. I mined these in Colorado myself."

"What?" Betty appeared distracted while her eyes narrowed and she rubbed her finger over a silver ring, focusing on the stone. She picked up a bracelet and held it to the overhead light, watching the silver sparkle and examining the rich blue and green turquoise hues. Her face broke into a smile. "Of course it's real!"

To Tessa's amazement, she reached over the counter and gave her a hug.

Tessa held her arms stiff to her sides, peering at Dillon in shock.

"I've been trying find you for months!" Betty burst. She released Tessa and wagged her finger. "Where have you been hiding? You're work is the best I've ever seen. One of my girlfriends brought in a necklace of yours six months ago, asking if I could find the amazing designer with the feather hallmark. And to think, that sleazy guy came in today and tried to pawn his jewelry off as coming from the same source. But look at this craftsmanship." She ran her finger along the elegant lines of Tessa's silver. "You can't fake it. I don't care if that man says his jewelry was the original brand—it's the *artist* I'm after."

"Well, he did employ me once," Tessa confessed, wanting to be transparent so Arthur couldn't skewer her with lies. "But after I left, I started my own line—"

"Thank God!" Betty pressed her hands to the counter. "That man—what's his name—Wackier? Jackier? He's a scumbag. He stared at my cleavage the whole time, like I don't have eyes. I was afraid to be alone with him and ready to call the cops, so I ordered him to leave." She turned Tessa's jewelry back over and scanned the designs, clapping her hands together. "Oh, I can't wait to tell Cassandra! You two will be here for a minute, right?"

Tessa nodded, glancing at Dillon.

"Fabulous!" Betty pulled out a cell phone and tapped a contact, waiting for the ring. "You won't believe this, Cassandra," she exclaimed. "I found her! Remember the feather designer? Well she's here, with a new line of jewelry. Her work is gorgeous—you've got to come over."

Betty drilled at contacts on her phone, calling more customers faster than Tessa could imagine. Within twenty minutes, people began pouring into *Midnight Serenade* to ogle her designs. They cooed over her silverwork that created a harmony between stone and bone, and soon they began to accost Tessa with giddy enthusiasm, asking where the turquoise and other elements of her jewelry came from. Their pointed questions became a clamor of noise, until Tessa cleared her throat loudly and waved her arm to get their attention.

"Everything comes from the Rocky Mountains," she assured them all with one global response. "And by the way, my inspiration and co-conspirator is standing right here." She beamed at Dillon. He gave her a proud nod, unperturbed by the buying frenzy that had ensued within the hour, when a camera crew suddenly burst through the front door.

"We're doing live streaming today for Spirit Fest," a reporter announced. "Getting all the action in Telluride this afternoon. And we couldn't miss the crowd that's been swarming into *Midnight Serenade*. There's a line out the door that reaches down the street. Tell me," he turned to Dillon and shoved a microphone in his face, "what brings you here today?"

Dillon's features remained granite as the reporter eagerly

awaited a response. He simply nodded at Tessa, who was busy holding up a bracelet and describing the particulars of her design to a small throng.

"Tessa Grove," Dillon said sharply over the din of customers. He turned to face her with admiration in his eyes. "The bravest woman I know."

Tessa ceased talking and set the bracelet on the glass case. She shot a glance at Dillon. As their gaze met, tears rimmed her eyes.

Within seconds, the reporter ditched Dillon and motioned for his camera crew to film her for their live stream. He sprinted to the counter and jammed his microphone at Tessa while the camera focused on a close-up. They recorded her for a few minutes, asking when she got started in the high-end jewelry business and how she developed her ideas. She tried her best to answer on the spot, looking like a deer in the headlights, until Betty interrupted the interview.

"Tessa!" She held up her cell phone with glee. "I got a call from Vega Fowler up on Benchmark Drive. You know, the woman who has her own fitness reality show? She saw you talking about your jewelry on TV just now, and she's wondering if you'd deliver? She already picked out a necklace and two bracelets and paid for them by phone. She's dying to meet you!"

Tessa nodded hesitantly, floored. "Uh, sure," she replied, a bit nervous. "Do you mean right now? While there are customers in your shop—"

"Oh, don't worry about a thing," Betty assured her. "I'll keep track of your sales receipts and take future orders, and we can do an artist meet and greet another time. Here," she wrote down the address to Vega's home on a piece of paper and handed it to her. "She's a real high roller who'll talk your work up to wazoo to her viewers." Betty leaned in and whispered, giving Tessa a wink. "Better get more inventory ready. Believe me, you won't regret going over to meet her."

Tessa's pulse raced, the air around her all at once feeling thick and heady. She grabbed an edge of the counter and inhaled a breath, unable to believe this was really happening. Her dream was coming true—in spectacular fashion! Staring down at the reflections on the glass, all she knew for certain was that she needed one thing to ground her.

Dillon—

When she swiveled around to search for him in the shop, his towering presence over the female shoppers made him easy to find.

Except he had a stern, far-away look in his eyes.

With a resignation on his face that sent chills down her spine.

Like a man going to war.

Tessa and Dillon rode the Telluride gondola to Mountain Village with the vintage traveling case containing Vega Fowler's purchases tucked against Tessa's chest. As they glided over the mountain top, her stomach twisted with nerves. The whole time, Dillon didn't say a word.

"Is this all too crazy for you?" she asked gently, hoping to break the ice. "I mean, I realize we just landed here, and everything took off like a rocket. I can hardly believe it myself." She chuckled a little. "Do you, um, need something to eat before we go to Vega's house?"

Dillon didn't reply, scanning the San Juan peaks around them that soared over 14,000 feet.

Tessa folded her hands together, feeling the need to fill the empty space with words. "You know, it is an exciting opportunity. Betty told me Vega Fowler's show is a blend of body and bling. She loves to rave about fitness and jewelry, and she'll talk up my designs. Think of it—I might actually need to hire employees."

Dillon stared straight ahead, oblivious to her enthusiasm. She couldn't tell if he was irritated or angry—or devoid of any feeling at all. His eyes had the fixed gaze of a man whose thoughts were rimmed by something buried long ago, which had never been allowed to see daylight.

As the gondola glided over private homes the size of premium hotels, Tessa resisted the urge to point at the stunning displays of architecture below them. Nothing she said seemed to enter Dillon's awareness. Finally, she became so worried she couldn't take it anymore.

"What is it?" She grabbed his knee and shook him. "You haven't spoken since we got in the gondola. Are you afraid of…heights? Tell me what's going on—"

When he shifted to face her, the ice in his eyes left her petrified. Yet there was something shadowy haunting the edges at the same time, as though he were staring down a long, dark tunnel with no possibility of return. To Tessa's mind, it looked like he was facing the Valley of Death.

All at once, a deep, disturbing sensation riddled her stomach.

Something inside Tessa told her she'd just been introduced to a figure she'd only ever heard about—

And his name was Big *Yi'yee.*

24

"I nearly killed him."

Dillon's flat tone scared her far more than the words he'd revealed. No longer did Tessa recognize this man. He was as half-frozen as the creek she'd fallen into that morning by the cabin, when Iron Feather had appeared to her.

With a splintered look in his eyes that appeared nothing short of deadly...

This is the man who's never lost a fight, she realized. Who could probably kill anyone on sight. Twisting her fingers, she stared at the floor of the gondola.

"Who are you talking about?"

Dillon didn't answer. He appeared to be searching the horizon over the mountains, replaying something in his mind.

"My last fight," he finally muttered. "I didn't know they had a house here."

When the gondola lurched at the end of its track, Tessa was left struggling for breath. It took everything in her to collect herself and maintain her balance as she stepped out. She backed away from the gondola, reeling.

His last fight? she thought. He must be talking about that man he put into a coma.

"Vega Fowler, is she—"

"Butch Fowler's wife," Dillon stated. "a.k.a. Baby Fat. The man who will never fight again."

Tessa linked her arm in his and tugged him from the gondola barn over to a nearby bench. She sat down beside him.

"Dillon," she felt her heart sink, "we don't have to do this. We can drop off my jewelry at the woman's doorstep and make an excuse for why we can't stay. She'll get over it. And it's all right if I lose future sales from her. Nothing is worth putting you through trauma—"

"It's not me who's traumatized," he said. "It's the boy."

"Boy?"

Dillon stared for a moment at the rustic gondola barn, listening to the eerie wail of the metal rollers against their cables. He watched gondola after gondola make the turn in front of them, only to head back over the mountain again. Round and round, never stopping.

He turned to Tessa.

Nervous, she wove her fingers together. Her grip tightened, waiting.

"Once, I was a fifteen-year-old boy," he began slowly, measuring his words, "who'd lost his parents to tragedy. Whose childhood was ripped from him, sentencing him to a life of anger."

Dillon's eyes met hers.

"I did that to another boy."

"What—how?" she said.

"Baby Fat's son. He was there that night. Watching his father go down. Watching their lives fall apart."

Tessa desperately wanted to comfort him. To tell him it wasn't his fault, and he didn't mean it. But the way Dillon's fists clenched to the point of shaking told her she was wrong.

He did.

And she was staring at the coldest side of Big *Yi'yee* in the face.

She inhaled a long, slow breath.

"Iron Feather told me," she said softly, "you need to use your talents for good. To heal. You can't unravel the past, Dillon. But at least you can go see that boy. I mean, if Vega Fowler will allow it."

Swallowing down the sharp pulse that had climbed up her throat, Tessa bravely squared her shoulders and looked Dillon in the eye. "You told me to face my fears back there at Betty's shop," she reminded him. "Well, I think it's time for you to do the same."

She paused to scan the San Juan Mountains, taking in the crystal blue sky so pure it appeared to reach to infinity. "This trip," she shook her head, goosebumps alighting on her skin, "feels like more than a sales venture. It's become," she chose her words cautiously, "a crossroads. For both of us. Don't you see that, Dillon? Whatever we do now," she hesitated, checking his eyes again, "directs our future. How much of our past we drag along."

Tessa sank her hands into her jeans pockets before inhaling a breath. "If nothing else, maybe you can just meet the Fowler boy and be present with him, with his pain. Even if he doesn't say a word, he'll know it took guts for you to do that. It might mean something to him."

"Or not." Dillon countered. He slanted his gaze to the rugged peaks that appeared impenetrable. "He's under no obligation to forgive me. To even meet with me."

"But this way, he *has* that opportunity. He'll always know you tried," Tessa urged. She fell quiet, listening to the relentless whine of gondolas that circled past them. She wanted to stop the grating sound, pull a lever that would make the motion cease. All she could do was remain seated on the bench beside Dillon while he weighed his thoughts.

Gradually, Dillon unraveled his fists and exhaled a breath. He grasped Tessa by the arm and rose from the bench, gently bringing them both to their feet. Then he turned and stared for a long while at the rays of sun that lit up the mountain tops, stretching into a late-afternoon glow.

When he finally took a step forward, Tessa had the distinct feeling he was leading her into the unknown. A kind of void where anything could happen. It could be beautiful, she thought, or very ugly. But whatever their experience turned out to be, as Dillon clasped her hand and escorted her toward the sunlit horizon, she knew something had been set into motion that neither one of them had the power to control.

Dillon and Tessa walked onto the cobbled driveway of the palatial mansion made of stone with thick timber accents. A man in uniform stood at the front door—a security guard, or some kind of servant. Tessa couldn't quite decide, but when the man saw them, he pressed a button on a console by the door and talked into it, nodding at the instructions he received.

"Tessa Grove?" he called out, motioning for them to come toward him. "We've been expecting you. Who's your guest?"

"Dill—"

Dillon bumped against Tessa, startling her. His arched brow told her not to reveal his name.

"Um…a *friend*," she stated.

With the touch of a passcode on the console, the man unlocked the front door with a heavy metal thud, as if a steel bar had been withdrawn from across a vault. Slowly, the door opened on its own, and the man walked in ahead of them.

Dillon paused, stealing a glance at Tessa. "When Vega sees me," he whispered, "she'll recognize me. No one forgets the man who made your husband a vegetable for six months. Things might get awkward fast, so be prepared. You may have to lay down your wares and leave."

"Okay," Tessa acknowledged, mustering the courage to lead the way over the transom into the foyer. She distracted herself by tilting her head at the giant chandelier above them with enough wattage to light all of Telluride. Lining the walls were bronze geometric sculptures with harsh angles and abstract paintings that looked more like roiled emotions hurled onto canvases. The artwork set her teeth on edge.

Nevertheless, the doorman gave them a warm smile. "Ms. Fowler will be down in a moment. She's very excited about meeting you." He disappeared into a side room.

On their own, Tessa and Dillon heard voices from above a grand staircase.

"Seriously, Mark? Fighting at school again?" A woman's brittle tone echoed from the second floor. "I don't have time for this! It's the third detention you've had in a month."

A blonde woman appeared on the landing in sleek, pink workout attire, toting a glass of Bourbon. She spun around to face a teenage boy with red hair behind her.

"Your grades are in the gutter. You keep picking fights! Doesn't your shrink help you figure out anything, with what we pay him?" She set her hand on her forehead with a pained expression. "Don't give me that look, Mark. It's high time you got into gear."

The woman sighed and began to storm down the stairs, when she spied Tessa.

"Oh my gosh, Tessa Grove?" She smiled, her eyes lighting up. "I'm Vega Fowler—welcome to our home!" She was so besotted with meeting the new jewelry designer that she didn't notice Dillon behind her.

"Mom," her son called out urgently, chasing after her on the stairs.

His mother had nearly reached the bottom when he yanked at her pink shirt to stop.

"MOM!"

Cross, Vega spun around. "For Christ's sake," she spit out, "what is it now?"

Her son's face had blanched to the color of the marble tiles at the base of the stairs. Speechless, he gripped his mother's shoulders and carefully rotated her to take a better look at her guests.

Vega's mouth slung open. She dropped her drink to the floor with a crash. Shards of glass scattered across the tiles, glistening in the chandelier light.

"Wh-what on earth are you doing here?" she stammered. "Mark, go get James and tell him to call the police—"

"Wait!" Tessa cut in. "I, um, I have your jewelry right here." She opened her case and held it up for Vega. "Dillon Iron Feather is my friend. He helped me design the pieces." She gazed into Vega's eyes. "He had no idea you lived here in Telluride—I swear."

All at once, a blur broke past Vega, charging toward Dillon.

"Mark!" Vega cried in horror, reaching after him. "No!"

Her son flung himself at Dillon with all his might, beating at him with his fists.

"You monster! You almost killed my dad!"

Dillon stood like a wall as the boy hammered at his chest and abdomen. His mother attempted to grab him, but it was no use. Mark shook her off with the fury of a wild animal. He kicked and wailed at Dillon as the doorman bolted back into the room. One look at Dillon's lethal gaze told him not to engage in this fight, so he pulled out a cell and began dialing. Dillon held up his hand with such a burning expression that he trembled and dropped the phone.

"I hate you!" Mark cried, drilling at Dillon until his knuckles were bloodied. "You ruined our lives!"

Dillon took the abuse with a peculiar tolerance that set Vega aback. Confused, she studied the way his arm muscles remained relaxed while Mark pounded him non-stop with everything he had. Dillon didn't retaliate in the slightest, and his lack of reaction made Mark only madder. Hot tears streamed down the boy's cheeks as his fists slowed with exhaustion. Yet he kept kicking in rage, drawing shallow breaths until he hyperventilated and crumpled to the floor. His agonized sobs made Vega dash to her son, motioning for the doorman to leave the room.

Dillon crouched down beside her. To Vega's wonderment, he wrapped his arms around the boy, rocking him back and forth. When Mark had gulped down enough air to finally regulate his breaths, Dillon gently lifted his chin and grasped his temples.

"Don't be like me, Mark. This anger, it destroys everything it touches."

"B-But you *deserve* to be destroyed!" Mark cried, sucking hard for air. His cheeks became beet red.

"There's a price no one tells you about."

"I don't care!" Mark protested.

"Yes you do," Dillon persisted. "Take it from me. Whoever you destroy lives inside you. Forever. I mean that, Mark."

The boy appeared stunned. His lips trembled like he'd been slapped in the face. He stole a glance into Dillon's eyes.

"What is this—some crazy fighter talk?"

"No." Dillon shook his head. "It's the truth. There isn't a goddamned day that goes by that I don't think of you and your father. Of the legacy of hate in your heart. A hate *I* created. And for what—a fighter's belt? I gave those away long ago. I want to see him, Mark."

"See him? You mean Daddy? Why would I—"

"Because he survived, in spite of me—in spite of the rage

inside. That's the strongest thing I've ever known a man to do. I want to see him with my own eyes, Mark."

The boy checked for his mother's reaction. Though tears streaked her face, Vega brought a shaky hand to her lips. She gave him a halting nod.

Mark wiped his eyes on his shirt, noticing the fabric had become bloody from his knuckles. He got up and walked ahead of Dillon, raising his chin to lead the way with some measure of adolescent dignity. Vega and Tessa followed behind them past the foyer to an area in the back of the house that was set up like a hospital room. White walls were stacked with medical equipment, and in the center was a large bed.

There sat Baby Fat, hooked to machines that pulsed with the rhythm of his lungs and heart. Though he was conscious, he appeared grayish and fifty pounds thinner, a fraction of his former self, with arm muscles wasted to thin, sinewy lines. The crimson mohawk was gone, his head shaved to a reddish stubble.

When he saw Dillon, his eyes stretched to twice their size. He edged his hand to a cord by his bed attached to a console that looked like it could sound an alarm.

The two men stared each other down.

For a moment, they seemed to be back in the Octagon again, sizing one another up. The pulsing beats of the machines began to wobble wildly. Vega gasped.

"No, it's too much for him!" she cried out. "We made a mistake—"

She lunged for Baby Fat's bed, when Dillon blocked her with his arm. He gently took hold of her shoulders to steady her and pointed to the red blips on a machine that were slowly settling to a more consistent rhythm. Baby Fat inhaled a deep, deliberate breath, glaring at Dillon.

Struggling, he lifted his feeble arm with a wince. He gave Dillon the finger.

"Asshole," he said in a hoarse voice. His other hand remained by the cord that he treated like a loaded gun.

Tessa's breath hitched—the fighter in this man was clearly still alive. All around the room, the air felt heavy and charged, and she feared Baby Fat might yank the cord to notify security.

Baby Fat grabbed an oxygen mask and pulled it to his face, sucking with labored breaths. His eyes became mere slits, but they never left Dillon for a second. "What the hell are doing here," he wheezed, his face flushed from the effort.

Dillon glared at him like a contender. With a measured silence, he allowed Baby Fat room for the kind of respect befitting a former champion. Slowly, he rubbed his hands over his knuckles, spreading his legs into a familiar fighter's stance. He cleared his throat.

"I'm here to finish the job, you idiot. Obviously my right hook didn't cut it."

Despite the fatigue on Baby Fat's face, a gleam surfaced in his eyes. "Damn straight," he seethed in a low, menacing tone. "And it never will." Gulping a few ragged breaths, his lips curled slightly, revealing a hint of a cocky smile. "Know why?"

Dillon smacked his fists into his palms, as though preparing for a round in the Octagon. He tilted his chin. "Why?"

Baby Fat slipped the mask over his face for another hit of oxygen. He took in several breaths before he forced out more words. "'Cause you're a no-count son of a bitch!" he replied. His body began to jiggle with hoarse laughter. Then he cradled his right arm and lifted it, bending at the elbow with his hand clenched. "I'll dust you."

"You wish." A trace of a grin tugged at Dillon's lips.

He boldly stepped up to the bed and sat beside Baby Fat, clutching his thin hand like a comrade. Dillon allowed him to arm wrestle and thrust his fist to the bedspread with a weak thump. Baby Fat released a raspy chuckle.

"Goddammit," Dillon sighed, glancing around the room. He toyed with medical wires and ran his hand along a throbbing machine. "I can't believe you conned me into paying your hospital bills, only to sit on your ass all day." He rolled his eyes. "What is this stuff, gold plated?"

"Platinum." Baby Fat gave him a pirate smile. He leaned over and threw his spindly arm around Dillon.

Tears slipped down Vega's cheeks, and she swiftly dabbed her eyes to try and hide her emotion. She backed away from the men, edging closer to Tessa. "Our old friends," she whispered in a low tone, so her husband wouldn't hear, "they, um, don't come around much anymore. This is the first visit he's had in months."

Tessa rubbed her arm and gave it a squeeze. "It won't be our last," she assured her. A lump swelled in her throat at the sight of the two men still lingering in an embrace. What was more startling was the expression on Mark's face—one of awe. Apparently, it hadn't escaped his attention that the men shared a history, a strange bond. Maybe, in their own weird way, they were two sides of the same coin.

When Baby Fat released Dillon, he regarded his son, motioning for him to come sit on the bed.

"Mark," he drooled a little, wiping his chin with his sleeve, "meet the biggest fricking loser in Colorado." He held up a fist to Dillon.

Dillon bumped it. "I can still whip your ass."

"Prove it," Baby Fat replied.

Mark appeared riveted, watching their repartee.

"Trash talk," his father said, grabbing the mask of oxygen for another draw. He breathed in long and slow. "Someday, you'll understand."

Vega walked to the side of her husband's bed and grasped a towel to wipe perspiration from his brows. "He tires easily," she cautioned, checking a clock on the wall. "He can only handle visitors for fifteen—"

"No!" Baby Fat protested, though his eyes appeared to droop. "Mark visits me for hours. Helps move my goddamned limbs."

The proud way his eyes embraced his son touched Tessa's heart. She shot a glance at Dillon, who gave the boy a pat on the back.

"I don't know how you, of all people, got a son like this," Dillon teased. "Better hang on to him."

"Y-You know," Vega offered, "Celia has some fresh pie in the kitchen." She scanned her visitors hopefully. "It's blackberry, made with local fruit."

Tessa waited for Dillon's reaction, knowing he never touched refined foods.

"We like ice cream on top," Mark pointed out.

"That'd be great," Dillon nodded, watching the boy bound eagerly from the bed to head to the kitchen.

As soon as he left the room, Baby Fat placed his hand over Dillon's on the bed. He clutched it and squeezed.

"Thank you," he whispered, watching his son disappear around the corner. Tears misted his eyes.

Dillon pulled him in for another hug.

"Any time, bro."

Baby Fat leaned back on a pillow and studied Dillon for a moment. He pointed a shaky finger at him, his eyes pained.

"I want you to know—"

He pulled the mask to his face and heaved a breath before continuing. He never took his gaze off Dillon.

"I wanted to kill you, too."

Dillon let his words hang in air, punctuated by the sounds of medical machines. His eyes narrowed at Baby Fat. Not in sympathy, but fighter to fighter.

"Part of you succeeded," Dillon replied.

He stared at Baby Fat's bony hand on the bed sheet.

"Now get off your ass and keep fighting." He turned to glance at Tessa before returning his focus to Baby Fat. "'Cause we're gonna come back here, you know." His eyes leveled on his former opponent. "Once a month, to check on you and make sure you're gaining strength and flexibility. I have a few tricks up my sleeve to help you rehabilitate. Even if my right hook does suck—"

Baby Fat burst into a strained laugh. Mark came back to the room with two plates of pie, dolloped with ice cream. He handed one to his father and one to Dillon. Vega tucked a towel under her husband's chin to keep the dessert from crumbling down his chest. Stabbing a fork into the pie, Baby Fat held up his plate.

"Cheers," he said.

Dillon speared a forkful and popped it in his mouth,

chewing awkwardly like it was laced with cough medicine. Baby Fat bit back a smile, swallowing his food with care. His son left the room and returned with more pie for Vega and Tessa.

"So, when are you going to get the hell out of this bed and go hunting with me?" Dillon asked. He scanned the medical equipment as though it were suspicious. "What do you think, Mark?" He eyed the teenager. "You ready to implement my ideas to help your dad get on his feet? That means you two will need to make serious progress each month before my visits, or forget the doctors. You're gonna have to deal with *me*."

"Sounds like a threat," Mark smirked, diving into a hunk of pie.

"Nope," Dillon replied with a glint in his eye. "Consider that a promise."

Mark downed a mouthful, gazing at Dillon with hope brimming in his eyes. "I, um," he said hesitantly, checking his dad's reaction. "I think I'd like that."

Though his father struggled to chew without drooling, he managed an awkward swallow. His eyes met Mark's.

"Me too, son," he said, dipping his fork into the vanilla ice cream. "Me too."

25

Dillon and Tessa arrived home in Bandits Hollow at midnight, grateful to enter the cabin and head for the wide, comfy bed. Tessa was so tired she could hardly think anymore, but the dizzying responsibilities of the day weighed heavily on her.

"We'd better get some shut eye," she yawned, stretching her arms. "With all the orders from Betty that came in, I need to hunt for more turquoise in the morning."

"Well, I need *you*," Dillon insisted.

He peeled off her shirt with a swiftness that took her by surprise and tossed it on the floor. Tessa giggled as he pulled her to him. She slid his shirt up his chest and yanked it over his head. Unclasping her bra, he freed her sumptuous breasts and wrapped his arms around her, skin on skin. His heartbeat throbbing against hers felt wonderful, just what she needed to come home to after a long day.

"I'm proud of you," Dillon whispered, dipping his head to kiss her lips.

There wasn't a hint of coldness in him any longer. It was as though Big *Yi'yee* had been transformed—and now it truly was just the two of them, two hearts, filling up the room. No intruders anymore.

"I'm proud of you, too," she echoed.

She tugged greedily at the top of his pants until she managed to wriggle the button free, unzipping and pushing them over his hips to the floor. Dillon did the same for her, and they laughed when they realized they were reduced to nothing but shoes.

"Time to get down to basics, mister," she warned, freeing her feet from her shoes and socks. "I want *all* your skin next to mine—now."

"Yes ma'am." He kicked off his boots and socks and stepped over to the dresser to put on a condom. When he returned, he enveloped her in a kiss, his hands seeking her hair, her delicate shoulders, the curve of her defined waist. He roamed his fingers over the luxury of her hips, pressing against her until she felt heat emanating from his palms. Tessa curled her leg around him, tantalizing him with the slide of her skin.

"I have to have you," he whispered, gripping her with a reckless desire that she wished with all her might she could bottle. It hungered for her, demanded her completely, and would do anything to have her.

They tumbled onto the bed and tangled in each other's limbs, all hands, lips, heat and electricity. Dillon rolled on top of Tessa, perched on his palms, his long hair spilling over his wide, muscular shoulders. Like he'd done before, he paused for a moment, his gaze taking in the full beauty of her face—tracing the shape of her forehead, nose, cheeks, lips—and those blue-green eyes that took his breath away.

"How did I get so lucky?" he said.

Tessa grasped his cheeks, her fingers resting against his rugged cheekbones. She peered into his eyes.

"Because you'll do whatever it takes to keep me," she winked.

Dillon didn't smile.

He didn't say a word.

His big brown eyes locked on hers with a determination that shook her.

"That is the truest thing you've ever said, Tessa Grove."

He dove for another kiss, pressing his broad, toned chest to her as though she were his life blood. He swiftly entered her, causing her to gasp. Tessa felt his force surge inside, filling up her senses with the woodsy male scent of his skin and the smooth, artful sway of his hips. Then he began to thrust deeper, stroking her in just the right places that left her hungry for more. Tessa grabbed fiercely at Dillon and collided their bodies, intoxicated by his hammering strength. She wanted to crush herself against him until they'd splintered into shining pieces, and all that was left was a fire between them that she'd gladly watch burn. Together they rocked hard, arousing swell after swell of pleasure that felt nothing short of magical. All at once, Dillon's brute power released a torrent of sensation inside her, reaching a wild pitch she thought might consume them whole. A sharp wail burst from Tessa's lips as ecstasy rippled through her, building until her cry of abandon sliced through the air like a blade. Panting for breath, her entire body trembled beneath Dillon, the heat between them blurring the edges of where she ended and he began.

And that's when she heard something…

Soft at first.

A bare hint of music.

Soon, light tones undulated in the air, the same way their bodies rose and fell in a sensuous rhythm only moments ago.

Dillon glanced at Tessa. There was an alertness in his eyes that told her he'd heard it, too.

Traces of notes, floating as light as feathers, seemed to come from near the dresser.

Tessa wondered if Dillon had a battery-operated radio in a drawer, or perhaps had left a cell phone there. His brows drew together and he shook his head, reading her thoughts. He got up from the bed and headed to the dresser. To her surprise, she saw his hand hesitate with a slight unsteadiness before opening the leather tie of his ancestor's suede pouch. He pulled a piece of turquoise from the medicine bag and studied it in his palm.

"Tessa," he said, turning around. "It's….warm."

"It's more than warm." She sat up and closed her arms around her waist, feeling her breath hitch. "It's…singing."

This is crazy talk! she thought, her heart racing. But when Dillon joined her on the bed, she couldn't ignore the tones that seemed to emanate from the stone.

They listened in silence to the notes that hummed lightly in air, as if dancing along the surface of their skin. He regarded the pouch on the dresser.

"I…I think I've heard this before," he confessed, reaching through the cobwebs of memory. "When I was little, long before reform school. Sometimes, when the sunlight came through our window, and my mother had fixed breakfast for us and gave us each hugs before school, we could hear soft notes rise in the kitchen between us. It was faint, but if you were quiet enough, you could catch the sound. My mother always kept this piece of turquoise on the table, and she'd smile at us when she heard it, too."

Dillon glanced at Tessa with a tenderness that astonished her. "She told us to always listen to the songs. They'd lead the way."

"Is this is the kind of magic Iron Feather had?" she asked cautiously. "T-Turquoise magic?"

Dillon grasped her hand and placed it over the stone in his palm. She felt a throbbing warmth from it like a beating heart.

"No," he said. He pressed his lips to hers for a kiss. "It's heart magic."

The next morning they loaded up their tools and went to the mine to unearth more turquoise. Tessa knew from her experience at Jacquier & Co. that the shades of the stone depend on the host rock found in the matrix as well as other minerals nearby, slowly transferring color through moisture over millions of years. The greenish-blue she'd found in a vein close to the entrance of her mine gained its color from iron. But the most vivid blue, the kind that looked as clear as the sky without a hint of green was usually found at greater depths, where copper is present. Tessa had a new bracelet in mind where a chunk of turquoise on top would represent sky and a polished slice of elk antler on the bottom would be earth. Grabbing a flashlight and a lantern, she'd persuaded Dillon to go deeper into the mine with her, hoping they wouldn't uncover too many spiders. Or worse, a rattlesnake or two.

As they walked forward in the darkness, Dillon barely had enough breathing room due to his height, making Tessa hope he wasn't claustrophobic.

"Guess miners in the nineteenth-century weren't as tall as you," she remarked with apology in her voice. "You're brave to go this far."

"It's okay." He swatted long strands of cobwebs from their path. "I figure once we reach the end, if we find a good vein, I can always come back later and carve out the walls more and add some supports."

That sounded like a great idea to Tessa, who'd noticed many of the old beams that bolstered up the mine appeared weathered and feeble.

After walking for several minutes, their flashlights and lanterns illuminated a rock wall before them—the end of the mine. Tessa scanned its surface, her gaze moving left and right, then dropping to the floor. She let out a gasp.

There, on the ground in front of her, was an old buffalo hide, rolled into a loose ball and covered in dust. She glanced at Dillon and peered at it warily, pulling out a mining pick from her backpack and using the handle to flip over the hide, as if it were vaguely dangerous and might conceal snakes. Dillon chuckled.

"I don't think it's going to bite," he pointed out. "Looks like it's been here over a hundred years. By the way, snakes can't survive where there's no water."

"Do you think a miner used it for a bedroll?" she asked.

"Maybe," he shrugged, until he spied something sticking out from beneath the hide.

It was an old cigar box, like the one Tessa's grandfather had bequeathed to her. The sight of the same green label on top gave her goosebumps. Only this one wasn't faded, probably because it hadn't seen daylight in a century. Tessa's curiosity got the best of her. She crouched on her knees and reached for the box, when Dillon's hand stopped her.

"Wait," he urged. He shone his flashlight directly on the cigar box.

The label on the top featured the face of a beautiful Victorian woman with long, flowing dark hair, marked by a peculiar streak of white. Beneath her image was written "Evangeline, 1895." A stamp under the label indicated the cigars had come by steamer ship from Havana. Dillon's face fell at the sight. He searched the ground for a moment, looking troubled.

"Evangeline?" he whispered. He glanced at Tessa and stooped to open the lid. Inside the cigar box was a yellowed sheet of paper, which he grasped and unfolded. It was a wanted poster for the Bandits Hollow Gang. The old photo featured a white man with the name *Virgil Hollow* printed beneath it. A Native American man stood beside him.

Iron Feather—

"Who's the guy next to your ancestor?" Tessa tapped the photo.

"Iron Feather's best friend," Dillon replied. "The two of them were the founders of the Bandits Hollow Gang." He picked up a few scattered pages that had been under the poster, scanning the florid cursive that appeared to have been written with a quill and bottled ink.

"These are love letters," he said softly.

"Whose?"

"Virgil Hollow's to Evangeline Tinker—the love of his life." He gazed at Tessa as though gauging how much information she could take. "Tessa," he placed his hand on her arm, "there's, well, a legend about those two."

Tessa met his gaze, intrigued.

"They say Evangeline Tinker could move through time—at will. With Iron Feather's help, she was brought to Virgil Hollow in 1895. The story goes that she assisted them with their robberies. I know this sounds…crazy. But some people claim she's alive right now. And that somehow, in a way we'll never grasp, Virgil Hollow still visits her."

Goosebumps spun across Tessa's skin. She took a deep breath to calm her careening heartbeat.

"Was she a…witch?" The mine suddenly felt darker to Tessa and potent with electric energy.

Dillon shook his head. "No one really knows. Except for the fact that Virgil and Evangeline were lovers." He held up the letters and gazed at Tessa. "Who could, well, manipulate…time."

Spooked, Tessa swallowed hard and hugged her arm around her waist. Yet she couldn't resist picking up the cigar box to see what had been beneath the love letters. Her fingers uncovered mysterious dried herbs and bones in small glass vials, a coyote's paw, and stones etched with small petroglyphs.

"I think it was Iron Feather who came in here," Dillon said, "to use the buffalo hide. This must have been his secret place." He tapped the papers in his hand. "He might have kept the letters to bring Virgil and Evangeline back, whenever he needed them. I mean, you know—if the legend is...true."

Dillon carefully folded the wanted poster and set it with the letters back inside the box. Tessa closed the lid.

At that moment, an owl's deep call echoed through the mine. It startled Tessa, making her drop her flashlight. The owl hooted again, and Dillon spotted something small and shiny to the right of them in the beam of light on the ground. Curious, he stepped forward to pick up the object and examine it. All at once, he gripped Tessa so hard at the shoulder that she winced in pain.

"Run!" he cried. His face had become the color of ash. "Now—"

Before she knew it, he'd gripped her by the arm and was practically dragging her with extraordinary strength toward the light at the opening of the mine. His feet moved at a pace that left Tessa breathless, clutching the cigar box at her side. When it became clear she couldn't possibly keep up, Dillon grabbed her around the waist and lifted her in his arms. He ran like their lives depended on it, chest heaving as his legs drummed beneath them. They barely reached the thin rays of daylight at the opening when a massive explosion rocked the mine. A black cloud of dust consumed Tessa and Dillon, blowing them several feet from the entrance, tumbling end over end.

Tessa's vision turned dark, as if a curtain had dropped before her. Slowly, she began to see stars twinkle across the sky with slow pulses of light. A voice called to her, echoing like the owl only moments before. She couldn't quite make out the words, when she saw a tall silhouette move in front of her, dark as a shade. In the starlight, she could barely see the outline of Dillon's features.

But it wasn't Dillon—

Tessa squinted, realizing from the old-fashioned hat on his head and the long black coat he wore that it was…

Iron Feather.

"What are you doing here?" she burst, frightened. "He's not cold anymore—"

He lifted his hand to bring her to silence. Tessa had to strain, narrowing her eyes to perceive something he held in his outstretched palm. In the weak light, she detected slightly blue hues. It looked to her like a piece of turquoise.

"Listen to the stones," he urged. "They'll protect you."

Feeling woozy, she searched her mind, recalling Dillon had said the Apache believed that turquoise protects their warriors.

"F-From what?" she asked.

Iron Feather turned his head in the darkness. On the horizon, the moon had risen over a mountain, making it appear a deep indigo. Slowly, the moon's radiance began to glow brighter, tinting the outline of the peak the same hue of the stone in his hand.

Turquoise Mountain.

Not far from Iron Feather, Tessa saw the silhouette of a large bear. Her breath halted, watching the massive animal lumber toward them. It appeared surly, swatting at tree trunks and turning over rocks to forage for food.

Iron Feather faced her and pressed the stone in her hand. It pulsed with warmth, with life.

"If you listen," he told her, nodding at the bear. "He will, too."

Confused, she was about to ask him another question when she felt a slap sting her cheek. She fluttered her eyes open and saw Dillon, bending over her in concern.

"Tessa! Can you hear me? Tessa—"

She blinked several times and sat up, watching the horizon keel in front of her. Glancing down, she realized she was covered in dirt, her arms wrapped tightly around the cigar box like it was a life preserver. She stared at Dillon, her eyes creased with questions.

"You okay?" He cupped her face, searching her eyes. He brushed his fingers over her forehead to check for bumps and pressed against her skull for bruises. There appeared to be no swellings.

Tessa wiggled her fingers a little and her shook her legs. "I think so. What on earth happened? A minute ago we were in the mine—"

Dillon held up a charred piece of wood that had been blown clear from the mine in the blast. Faint red letters across it spelled *Dynamite*. Tessa studied the word, flabbergasted.

"People come across old stashes of dynamite in mines around here all the time," he said. "They're from the gold rush over a hundred years ago, and most of the nitroglycerin would have seeped out by now. I'm not saying dynamite's ever safe to fool around with, but there's no way it could have created an explosion like this."

"Th-Then what did?"

Dillon drew a heavy breath. "When we were inside and you dropped your flashlight, I spotted something shiny on the ground. The second I stepped over to pick it up, I brushed against a suspicious tight cord on the ground—the kind used for a trip wire. This was the object I pocketed."

He held out his hand to her. On his palm was shiny cuff link. Tessa picked it up and turned it over. There, on the top, were the letters *AJ* stamped in gold.

She bowed her head to her knees and began to scream.

26

Blue and red lights from Barrett's cruiser swirled angrily as he sped down the road, roiling clouds of dust. He halted his vehicle before the ranch gate and didn't wait for Dillon to walk out to open it, dashing out the door and vaulting over the fence. Running until he reached Dillon and Tessa on the cabin porch, his dark eyes appeared pinched in concern. Nevertheless, he looked them up and down.

"Whoa, you guys are filthy!"

Despite his outburst, Tessa could tell he was worried sick about them.

"We're *alive*," replied Dillon.

"You got nine lives, bro." Barrett shook his head as he pulled out a note pad from his jacket pocket, shooting a glance at the rubble blown several feet from the mine. "Tell me what's been going on—I'll file a report right away."

"What you see is what you get." Dillon tipped his head to

the mine. "We got caught in one hell of a blast. I accidentally crossed a trip wire when I found this cuff link in the mine." He held up the gold link and dropped it in Barrett's hand. "Like I told Tessa, there may be old dynamite around here, but there was no reason for miners to use trip wires a century ago when they had perfectly good blast boxes. Someone set us up, Barrett. Tessa has a pretty good idea who it is."

Barrett finished scribbling and turned to her, his pen poised in anticipation.

"I saw my former boss from a New York jewelry firm in Telluride the other day." She hugged her elbows, hardly believing her own words. "And then we found this cuff link in my mine. It has his initials on it—*AJ* for Arthur Jacquier. I spotted the exact same piece of jewelry on him a while back, on the day I quit."

Barrett's eyes narrowed. "Are you implying your boss from the East Coast trailed you here? Why would he do that?"

"Gold," Tessa replied without hesitation. "When I worked for Arthur, I knew he was always striking deals for precious metals, since their prices are so high. Some of his transactions started to look, well, shady. Especially at the end when most of the gold I worked with came in unmarked shipments from Colorado—with no name of a mining company anywhere to be found." She stared at Barrett before darting her gaze to the mine. "Frankly, I think Arthur Jacquier has been in league with Bill Crouch all along. I just didn't know it. Now the easiest way for them to keep profiting from illegal gold mining is to get rid of me—and Dillon."

Barrett's eyebrows creased in skepticism. Yet when he studied the weathered floorboards of Dillon's porch for a moment in thought, he nodded as though it began to make sense. "So," he conjectured aloud, "you figure Arthur and Bill want you two gone…so you won't witness them using Tessa's mine to reach the new gold vein that was uncovered near here?"

"Exactly," Dillon said. "Bill Crouch already offered Tessa sixty grand to take the mine off her hands—I was there. She turned him down cold, so the blast was apparently his next idea."

"Amazing," Barrett muttered under his breath. He patted Tessa on the shoulder, releasing a cloud of dust. "Good thing you're okay." He scribbled several more lines on his notepad. "But I guess the big question is, where is this Jacquier guy now?"

"Probably at the only hotel in town," Dillon replied. "The Golden Wagon Hotel."

"Nell's place?" Barrett said, floored. "Wouldn't that be pretty obvious, if you suspect him of laying the trip wire?"

Dillon smiled. "He doesn't know we found his cuff link, bro. He might not even realize it's missing. From what Tessa's told me, he's the type of jerk who'd never imagine people are smart enough to be onto him."

"My favorite kind of criminal." Barrett tucked his notepad back into his jacket and slung his thumbs from his front pockets. "What say we pay ol' Nell a visit and see how she's doing at the hotel? If we're lucky, we might score some Angus burgers for lunch."

∽

After Dillon and Tessa got cleaned up, they went with Barrett to see Nell in Bandits Hollow. The moment they opened the door and entered the lobby, she let out a howdy that could shake the rafters. She'd heard the gossip from Betty about Tessa's success in Telluride, and her face was overcome with pride.

"I knew you'd nail it!" Nell beamed, giving her a big hug. She glanced down at the necklace Tessa had given her around her neck. "How could you not," she held up the silver pendant, "with craftsmanship like this?"

Tessa smiled. "I hardly know how to thank you for sharing your connections with me," she gushed. "Honest, it's changed my life. And on the subject of Telluride connections," she grasped Nell gently by the shoulders and peered into her eyes, "we saw someone while we were there. Someone who we suspect is responsible for engineering an explosion in my mine."

Nell's eyes shot open wide. "Explosion?" She looked Tessa up and down. "Are you all right, honey?"

"I'm fine," Tessa assured her. "The mine's going to need a lot of work, but no real harm done. Nell," she nodded for Barrett to hold out the gold cuff link, "have you seen a skinny, middle-aged guy lately who wears designer suits and flashy bling—"

"Who stares at every woman's cleavage within a fifty-mile radius and is a really crummy tipper?" Nell set her hand on her hip. "Sweetie, he's a bit hard to miss! In fact, he's staying in room number ten. But he headed out early this morning."

Nell leaned into Tessa's ear. "If you're thinking about

confronting him, make sure you carry my pistol, okay? That man has issues."

"Got it right here," Tessa whispered, patting the bulge on her hip.

"What we need is evidence and his location," Barrett cut in. "I haven't had time to get a search warrant. Any idea where he might have gone for the day?"

"All I know is that he met that snake Bill Crouch in my restaurant for breakfast. They sat at a table for over an hour and doodled all over a napkin without even bothering to leave a tip."

"Napkin?" Barrett looked intrigued. "You mean one of those cloth red bandana ones? What did you do with it?"

"Threw it away. They used pens, and the ink wasn't going to wash out, so the napkin's in the dumpster out back."

"Public domain," Barrett smiled, looking like he'd won the lottery. "Do me a favor, Nell. Set aside the receipt for their breakfast that has the date and time they were here. And tell Kit I'll ask her a few questions about their visit later. Mind if I investigate your dumpster?"

"Why, Barrett Iron Feather," Nell smiled, "I never pegged you for a dumpster diver."

"You'd be amazed at what I'll do to crack a case," he replied with a sly grin. He glanced at Dillon and Tessa. "Come on," he urged, unbuttoning the cuffs of his blue uniform. "Let's roll up our sleeves and raid the trash."

∼

"Garbage tells no lies." Barrett held up a torn dishtowel, drizzled yellow from what appeared to be mustard or eggs.

"Maybe not, but it sure as hell stinks." Tessa had to bite the insides of her cheeks not to lurch. The smell inside the dumpster was horrendous. They'd borrowed food-service gloves from the restaurant to do their search, and she dearly wished they'd snagged a few clothespins from the hotel laundry room to pinch off their noses as well. In the large dumpster was a sea of trash bags and crumpled hotel sheets that had seen better days, tossed to make way for new linens. Since it was two in the afternoon, and Nell had told them the restaurant takes out the garbage around noon and at closing, it was safe to assume the breakfast trash was in one of the bags on top.

"I found a receipt," Dillon piped up, holding a limp piece of paper marked with coffee stains. He squinted at the faint printing. "It's a customer copy—the date's today, and the time is 8:32 AM." He pointed to the black plastic he'd ripped open. "So this must be the right bag."

"Excellent, bro!" Barrett gave him a fist bump. He tossed aside the dish towel and stepped carefully over a mound of trash to Dillon's bag, crouching down to rip it open wider. He gently rifled through the garbage, his face brightening when he pulled out a red bandana.

"Hello, evidence!" he said, holding the bandana by the corners to the sunlight. Scrutinizing the fabric, he turned to show Dillon and Tessa. "What do you make of these pen marks?"

Tessa and Dillon peered closer, observing an X at the center of the cloth connected by long lines that might be construed as roads. At the top of the bandana was an N and on the bottom an S, with a W and an E on the left and right.

"Looks like a map," Dillon observed. He pointed to some jagged marks. "These could be mountains to the north and west of the X. The wavy lines are probably a river or creek." He fell quiet for a moment, sifting his thoughts. "The only place I know that has topography like that is Whiskey Gorge." He glanced up at Barrett. "You know, that old mining road we used to play on as kids. It's bordered on the north and west by mountains, and the road winds past Findler Creek."

"The one that has an old mine on it that mom warned us never to go into?" Barrett nodded. "How convenient. If Jacquier and Crouch are still trying to find a way to tap into the new gold vein, it'll do the trick."

Tessa leaned forward to examine the marks on the bandana. When she spied handwriting on the bottom right-hand corner, her eyes popped. She pointed a trembling finger to the fabric. "Whoa, look at this—"

On the fabric, scrawled in nearly illegible letters, appeared to be a list. It said:

More dynamite

Tunnel boring machine

Hire three extra workers

Make sure Tessa Grove & boyfriend dead

The sight of those words riddled her with shock. Tessa gripped Dillon's shoulder as reality sank in—

So Arthur really *had* intended to kill her. He was not merely sleazy; he was as dark a criminal as they come.

Barrett pulled out his cell phone and took a close-up photo of the writing on the bandana. "I'll put this evidence in zip lock bag when we get to the car," he assured her.

"There's not exactly a name on it," Tessa replied. "How can you prove this is the work of Jacquier and Crouch?"

"Gold," Barrett said with an unwavering stare. "Ironically, the very thing they're after is what will expose them." He turned over the bandana until he found a tag. "This cloth is seventy-percent polyester. Which means it's a pretty good candidate for a VMD test, where they use a thin film of gold to detect fingerprints on fabric. Technology is amazing these days."

"But you need people to catch criminals." Dillon lifted his gaze to the position of the afternoon sun, still high over the nearby mountains. "We have enough time to find them, if we head out now."

"Roger that," Barrett replied.

"Can we reach the mine in your police car?" Tessa asked. "Or do we have to saddle up horses?"

"Sweetheart, there ain't no *we* about it," Barrett insisted. "My cruiser can make it there on backroads, but you're not going. If these guys are caught doing anything illegal, Crouch's men wouldn't think twice about shooting you. Or me, for that matter. I doubt Jacquier is much better."

"But Arthur Jacquier came after *me*!" Tessa burst. "He tried to destroy my mine and my dreams." She blushed at the volume of her outburst, but she couldn't help it. "I want to be there to see this finished right. Besides, you can't deny I'm an expert witness. Show me his cuff link again."

Barrett dug into his shirt pocket and pulled out the piece of gold.

"Now turn it over."

He did as she asked, revealing beneath the monogrammed cuff link a tiny image of a feather.

"I *made* that cuff link," she said, glaring at Barrett and Dillon. "That's my hallmark from my days working jewelry in New York. If Arthur is still wearing the other one, I can identify it as an exact match on the spot and serve as a witness for his immediate arrest."

Barrett shifted his gaze to his brother. "She's stubborn, ain't she?"

"And brave as hell," Dillon replied. "Look Barrett, from what I've seen, Tessa will go up there whether you want her to or not. So you might as well take her up on her offer, as long as she stays safe in your cruiser." He turned and regarded Tessa's face with a mixture of admiration and worry. "Promise me," he pressed in a tone that bordered on threatening, "when we reach Whiskey Gorge, you'll remain in the car, all right?" He leaned in close to whisper in her ear. "And don't be afraid to pull that gun if you have to."

Tessa's cheeks prickled. *Of course* Dillon had spotted Nell's pistol slipped inside the waistband of her jeans. And as much as she wanted Arthur to go to jail for a very long time, part of her was still anxious at the mere thought of seeing him. He was devious beyond comprehension, and there was no telling what he'd do to guard his sources of gold. Drawing a deep breath, she searched the two men's eyes.

"I promise," she said.

27

The route to Whiskey Gorge was tortuous with sharp turns and deadly drop offs, a dirt backroad that hadn't been graded in years. Barrett raced down it anyway, calling for back-up to follow him. Another police car arrived at the unmarked junction where the side road to the abandoned mine veered to the left. Barrett slowed down and told his fellow officer via car radio that they had to creep the last quarter mile so their dust wouldn't reveal their position. Then he reached to the ceiling above his rearview mirror for the control module to turn on his in-car video system.

"If you look next to my mirror," he mentioned to Dillon and Tessa in the backseat, "you'll see my camera lens facing forward. I'll be leaving it on from here on out to catch the action—and everyone who's involved."

Tessa felt sharp tingles sprint down her back—this stakeout was really happening. She could hardly believe law enforcement was chasing down her former boss for attempted murder, let alone illegal mining. She nodded at Barrett, when she heard him clear his throat.

"Listen, I don't care how concerned either one of you are about this case," he warned. "You're both staying in the car. Things could get nasty real fast, and I can't be responsible for civilians getting shot. Got it?"

Dillon said nothing while Tessa chewed her lip. Barrett pressed down the road, crawling at a snail's pace, until he reached a bluff. According to the GPS map on his mounted mobile computer, the abandoned Whiskey Gorge mine appeared to be around the corner. He stopped the vehicle and let the engine idle. Then he went to the back and opened up the trunk, pulling out a semi-automatic rifle.

"AR-15," Dillon nodded appreciatively, glancing at Tessa. "My brother's got some pretty cool toys."

"You guys must have ice in your veins," she sighed. "Who cares about his toys when he's about to go up against criminals—"

"Tessa," Dillon settled a hand on her knee. "Barrett *lives* for arresting men like this. It's his idea of a perfect day—especially since you can identify Arthur's other cuff link. Believe me, if Barrett hadn't become a cop, he would've sought out fights all his life, just like me."

"Great," she shook her head, wondering if all the Iron Feather brothers were crazy.

She watched a police officer with another rifle walk up to join Barrett, and the two of them talked about strategy before high-fiving each other. Then Barrett ducked his head into the vehicle window.

"Dillon," he instructed, "as soon as we sneak around that

bluff, I want you to put a black tarp over the hood of this vehicle so none of the shine from the chrome tips them off in daylight. Then pull the car up to the shadows, just far enough to see the mine. That way the camera will catch everything."

"Will do," Dillon agreed.

Barrett disappeared around the bluff, and Dillon stepped out and retrieved a tarp from the trunk, laying it over the hood. He got into the driver's side and inched the cruiser forward into the shadows, then killed the engine.

Before them, down a short dirt drive, was the gaping hole of an old mine supported by rustic wood beams. Several construction vehicles were parked outside—the same ones they'd seen before—while Crouch's men were sitting on the ground eating a late lunch. A rail car appeared at the entrance of the mine, and Tessa startled when she saw Arthur Jacquier and Bill Crouch emerge from the darkness and stand beside it. They were smiling and slapping each other on the back.

"Must have reached the motherlode," Dillon observed. "The new vein was discovered only about half a mile from here. I bet they blasted their way into the other side of it to tap into the gold."

Dillon got out of the car and reached through the back window to cup Tessa's cheek.

"You stay here, like Barrett said. Or I swear I'll come back and hog-tie you again and throw you in the trunk." He gazed at her sternly and reached into his pocket, pulling out the piece of turquoise that once belonged to his ancestor and dropping it in her hand. "Hold onto this," he said mysteriously, as if it were a talisman for good luck. "I'm heading down the other side of that hill to the mine, in case Barrett gets in trouble."

"What?" Tessa protested. "He told us *both* to stay planted."

A sharp tenderness surfaced in Dillon's eyes, the depth of which took Tessa by surprise.

"I gotta protect my brother," he insisted. "It's what I've done my whole life, ever since my parents died. I'd never be able to live with myself if something happened to Barrett or Lander."

Tessa's breath hitched. The love Dillon had for his brothers left her speechless, unable to argue with him. She watched him grab another rifle from the trunk of the cruiser, completely unauthorized by law enforcement, and snag a magazine of ammo. As much as Tessa wanted to stop him, she could hardly blame Dillon for what he was about to do.

He returned to her car door and opened it, leaning inside to swipe a kiss.

"I love you, Tessa Grove." He gazed into her eyes with a fierce vulnerability that sent her heart into a spiral. "Now you stay here," he pressed his strong hand against her cheek, "and don't do anything stupid."

With that, Dillon quickly shut the door before Tessa could reply and made his way in the opposite direction, following another deer trail to keep a keen eye on his brother. The windshield of the police car was caked in dust, making it nearly impossible for her to see, so she climbed out of the vehicle to get a clearer view.

"I love you too, Dillon Iron Feather!" she vowed to the air, her heart twisting into a knot as she watched the three men close in on either side of the mine. Goosebumps skittered on her skin when Arthur Jacquier and Bill Crouch sat down to eat lunch with the workers, having no idea who was about to ambush them. To Tessa's astonishment, one of the workers got up and unloaded a case of dynamite from a Jeep, then took it to Arthur and Bill and set it carefully on the ground. He returned to the Jeep and whistled for the rest of the crew to join him. When they drove off, Arthur and Bill gave them a wave.

"Guess they're not allowed to be near dynamite," Tessa muttered under her breath, craning to see a little better.

"Nope," a low voice replied behind her as a rough hand sealed her lips. Tessa felt the barrel of a pistol shove against her skull, pressing to bone so hard she cried out. Her scream was muffled by the stranger's palm. "It's against code to let ranch hands detonate explosives without training. But Crouch don't give a shit." The man laughed. "He just wants to make sure they don't do something stupid. Like blast the gold vein to pieces."

Tessa wriggled with all her might and kicked him hard, landing her heel against his knee and sending him stumbling backwards in pain. She swiveled and pulled Nell's pistol out from her hip, but he beat her with his aim. His gun was already pointed at her forehead.

"Hot damn, you're feisty!" The man cried, shaking his hurt leg. "Now drop that weapon, or my ugly face is the last thing you'll ever see."

Trembling, Tessa let Nell's pistol fall to the dirt. "Wh-Who are you?" she demanded.

"Crouch's foreman." He flashed her a crooked smile. "He's got a right to know some girl with a gun was watching from a police car. Lucky for him, I went to the creek over there to fetch more water for lunch and caught your ass." He nodded at a jug and a filter that sat beside the creek bank. "Now cough it up—where are your friends?"

"F-friends?"

He smacked her across the cheek with the pistol, making her skin burn.

"Don't act stupid, bitch. There's two police cars here, which means you've got company." He grabbed her shoulder and spun her to face the mine. "Show me exactly where they are."

Tessa bit the inside of her cheeks, refusing to be intimidated. With a shaking hand, she pointed in the opposite direction of Barrett and Dillon. "Over there, on that hill," she lied. "See that ridge? That's where they're watching from a hideout."

"Oh yeah?" The man gave her a hard shove to walk in front of him on the dirt drive. "How about you go tell Crouch that yourself?"

Heart pumping out of control, she marched ahead of the foreman, afraid to peek behind her as she made her way down the uneven dirt road to the mine. She knew Barrett and Dillon had probably seen her already from their hiding places that flanked the mine entrance, but she resolved not to lift her gaze and tip off where they were. Swallowing deep breaths, she prepared for the inevitable—for Arthur to recognize her, and then hear from the foreman that he'd caught her in a police car. For all she knew, Arthur or Bill might shoot her on the spot.

When she and the foreman neared the mine, Bill tapped Arthur on the shoulder and pointed at them. Arthur swung around. He began to laugh.

"Well, well—Tessa Grove!" he called out. "We meet again. You never cease to surprise me. Don't tell me you wanted to prospect for gold here, too?"

"Oh, it gets worse than that," the foreman replied. He grabbed Tessa by the hair and dragged her to within inches of Arthur and Bill. "I found her in a police car by a bluff back there, near the creek. There was another police car behind her." He narrowed his gaze. "Which means this place is crawling with cops." He shot a glance at the ridge Tessa had pointed to. "So unless y'all get down here right now," he called in a big voice, pressing his pistol harder to Tessa's temple, "I'm gonna blast this pretty thing's head off."

"No!" Tessa cried out to Barrett and Dillon, her voice echoing off the nearby hillsides. "It's too late—get out of here!"

The foreman struck her again with his pistol, using such force this time she dropped to the ground before he returned his aim to her head. "I highly suggest you come out of hiding," he yelled at the top of his lungs, "unless you want to dig her grave today."

By this time, Tessa realized Arthur and Bill had pulled out guns as well. Of all the absurdities, she noticed the handle of Arthur's handgun appeared to be encrusted with sapphires. The sight made her want to vomit. Her vision became blurry for moment from the blow to her head. As her eyesight settled, she spotted Barrett and the other police officer from their positions on the deer trail, holding their rifles above their heads.

But where was Dillon?

All at once, she recalled that there was no reason for Arthur, Bill, or the foreman to know Dillon was there.

Barrett and the other officer walked carefully down the hillside toward the men with their rifles held high. When they reached the mine, Barrett caught Tessa's gaze. His eyes didn't betray a hint of fear as he and his fellow officer tossed their rifles to the ground.

"Who tipped you off about our mining?" Bill demanded, pointing a gun at Barrett while Arthur aimed at the other policeman. He nodded at Tessa. "That bitch? How did she know—"

"She had a map of all the nearby mines, scoping out the competition," Barrett lied, sparing Nell for the tip she'd given them about the marked napkin. "She figured this one would interest you the most. A wild guess—"

"Wild guess, huh?" Bill replied. "I'll show you something wild—Tom, take her and these men deep in the mine. We were gonna blast one more time this afternoon anyway. When we're done," he eyed the case of dynamite, "there won't be a thing left for coroners to find." Bill glared at Barrett. "Now move—"

Before those words had completely left Bill's lips, a shot rang out that made a burst of red explode over his heart and felled him to the dust. Within seconds, another shot took out the foreman. Tessa reeled at the accuracy of Dillon's aim, but she and Barrett and his partner dove for the guns on the ground anyway. Despite the fact that they held weapons in their hands and scrambled to their feet, Arthur had already seized the moment and thrust his pistol between Tessa's eyes.

"Not so fast, my Number One." He wrapped an arm

around her and dragged her in front of him as a human shield, facing the direction that Dillon's shots had come from. "Is that your Cro-Magnon boyfriend out there?" he hissed. "You were a fool to leave Jacquier & Co." He licked her cheek in a creepy display of dominance that set her teeth on edge. "Because this is how it's going to end—with you and your friends dead."

"Face it!" He called out at full volume to Dillon. "Unless you get your ass down here in thirty seconds, I'm killing her."

Dillon emerged from the foliage of the deer trail, rifle held high like his brother's had been. He walked toward Arthur with a burning glare in his eyes, every muscle in his thick arms flexed, appearing formidable. Arthur's arm against Tessa trembled, but his fear only made him jam his gun that much harder to her temple. When Dillon arrived in front of them, he tossed down his rifle. Arthur motioned for him and Barrett and the other officer to go into the mine.

"Get inside," he barked.

After Barrett and his partner filed into the mine, Dillon lingered, glaring not at Arthur, but at Tessa. Far from heartbreak, his gaze implored her with an urgency of something else—an intense reverence she recalled seeing only on their hunting trip. All at once, she felt the piece of turquoise he'd given her that she'd put into her pocket start to burn against her skin. It throbbed against her hip bone, as though ignited by some kind of otherworldly energy. For the life of her, she thought she could hear faint music.

"I said, get in the mine!" Arthur ordered. He appeared oblivious to the notes that lifted from Tessa's pocket, and he raised his gun and fired a shot at Dillon. The bullet ricocheted off a thick stone beside the entrance of the mine. Dillon didn't flinch.

Turquoise, Dillon's lips mouthed the word as he gazed at Tessa one more time. His eyes didn't appear to have an ounce of fear—only faith that she might know what he meant. Before Arthur could shoot again, Dillon had slipped into the mine, disappearing into the darkness.

"Finally!" Arthur huffed, fondling the top button of Tessa's shirt until he managed to get it open. "No reason to waste these curves before they meet their maker." Arthur spun her to face him. His leering gaze left no doubt in her mind about his intentions. He tore at the next button, ripping it off and tossing it to the ground. "Like I told you before," he laughed, "you're a dime a dozen."

Rage surged through Tessa's bloodstream, when she heard more than simply notes. A song drifted from the stone in her pocket. At the same time, a rhythmic flow of words began to echo from the mine. The language was unfamiliar, but she was pretty sure it was Apache. It was then she realized it came from Dillon.

He was singing—

A slow chant that matched the melody from the stone.

Tessa yanked the turquoise from her pocket, ignoring Arthur's wayward hands that had descended to her breasts. She held the stone with all her might and attempted to sing the words, no matter how crazy that seemed. Arthur was so busy trying to tear off her shirt with one hand and his pistol in the other that he didn't notice the silhouette that appeared on the nearby ridge.

It was a bear.

Large and black, like the one that had appeared to her with Iron Feather, moments after the mine explosion. Shaking, Tessa kept trying to sing the words, until she heard a voice trail over the ridge. It sounded a bit like Dillon's, only older. The goosebumps that alighted on her skin told her it was Iron Feather's.

You are marked by the bear, shich'choonii.
We can hear you.

At that moment, she saw the bear stand up in the distance. It began to charge.

And so did Dillon.

With incredible speed, the bear tore over the brush and down the hillside in great bounds. In shock, Arthur shot at the animal and missed. His shaking hand immediately attempted to fire again, but the bullet ricocheted off a tree. Within seconds, the bear was nearly upon them. Just before it leaped in attack, Dillon made it to Tessa's side and whisked her away. He held her tight in his arms as the animal began to maul Arthur, diving for his throat. Barrett and the other officer retrieved their guns, spotting the pistol Arthur had dropped, now too far from his grip. They stood and watched while the bear ripped him to pieces.

Dillon continued to softly chant the Apache song in Tessa's ear, covering her eyes so she wouldn't have to witness the gruesome scene. Tessa forced away his hand.

"I want to see," she insisted.

By the time she shoved aside Dillon's fingers, however, the bear was gone. Barrett and his partner stared at Tessa, wide-eyed, like they'd seen a ghost.

The music from the turquoise in her hand had stopped.

All Tessa could hear was the sound of an owl in the distance. Its call threaded through the air with a haunting cry that echoed over the ridge.

Beside Arthur's body, which was bloody and mangled on the ground, was a long, white feather.

28

"Dillon, there's something you never told me," Tessa said as she swayed in his arms while he led her in a surprisingly artful waltz. She was wearing a long dress that Nell and Kit had found for her, made of turquoise-colored silk that fit tightly to her narrow waist and highlighted her eyes. Dillon had on a classic black tuxedo that accentuated his wide chest and broad shoulders.

"What's that?" he replied, moving his body with hers in a manner that was downright suave. He pulled her closer to him.

"How'd you become such a good dancer?" she smiled. A blonde lock fell tantalizingly down her cheek from her swept-up hair.

"My fighting career," Dillon replied. "You train for years to glide with power without wasting energy. You know, floats like a butterfly?"

Tessa nodded as she gazed over the crowd dressed in formal attire in the massive ballroom of Lander's mansion.

He had decided to throw a fundraising party for local law enforcement in appreciation for the way they'd recently helped Tessa and Dillon. But she half-suspected the real reason was so Lander could use the event as an excuse to meet the prettiest women in the county. She enjoyed watching him talk them up in their candy-colored ball gowns, looking dapper in his custom-made tuxedo. Barrett, on the other hand, appeared supremely uncomfortable standing alone in a corner, until one of Lander's staff offered him a flute of champagne from a silver tray. She was a lovely brunette in a black uniform, and her ability to chat him up made his eyes soften a little. Tessa had to admit, those Iron Feather brothers certainly looked dashing in their formal wear.

Dillon continued to guide Tessa seamlessly into another waltz while the orchestra began playing a new piece. As they moved across the ballroom floor, he flashed Nell a smile, admiring her bright red gown and the handsome cowboy with silver hair she'd snagged to dance with. Then he tilted his head a little with his brows furrowed, studying Tessa.

"But that's not really what you wanted to ask me, is it?" His eyes searched hers, detecting unease. "What's bothering you?"

Damn, she thought, cheeks tingling. She never could keep anything from him—Dillon always managed to read her like a book. Tessa peered into his eyes.

"I know you'd like to put it behind you," she said delicately. "But after Barrett and his partner loaded Arthur's body into the police car last week," she hesitated, recalling the grim details that were the stuff of nightmares. "I...um...I never saw any bear tracks. I mean, all I saw were your footprints near the body, after you ran from the mine to save me."

"Oh?" Dillon whirled her into another waltz circle, but his tactic for distraction didn't work.

Tessa tugged his chin to face her head on and gazed into his eyes. "Tell me the truth," she pressed. "I heard a rumor that no bear was seen on the footage from the police camera, either. The only thing left beside the body was an owl feather—"

The loud clanging of a bell pierced the room. "Dinner time!" Lander cried, motioning for his guests to approach the buffet table.

Though the chandeliers and gilded walls of the ballroom rivaled Versailles, that didn't stop Lander from wearing a cowboy hat and boots along with his tux and having a spread of chili and cornbread set out for his guests. Everyone in the ballroom broke from their waltz and began to crowd the long table, ready for hearty chow.

Tessa noticed that Nell and her beau were the first in line. She sighed, figuring she would have to ask Dillon about the odd circumstances surrounding the bear later, when she felt him link his arm through hers and gently escort her away from the buffet.

"Wait, what are you doing?" she protested. "I'm starving! It's not every day I get to try the cuisine of Lander's Parisian chef—"

"You mean the elk chili and cornbread?" Dillon laughed. "I think I'd rather rely on my time-honored game recipes than some fancy French imitation. Don't worry, we'll get to dinner soon enough."

Nell had turned from the buffet table with a plate of food in her hands and spied Dillon, giving him a nod with a glint in her eye. Dillon's chest swelled in response, and with a big smile, he whisked Tessa toward the center of the ballroom. Under a gigantic chandelier, he bowed on one knee and pulled out the old cigar box they'd found in her mine. Tessa wasn't quite sure, but she thought she saw his eyes mist up.

"Tessa Grove," he said softly, "you captured my heart the first day I saw you. Beyond your beauty, your soul has the strength of Turquoise Mountain, which my mother foresaw long ago. And what I want to know now is…will you be mine forever?"

He lifted the cigar box to her hand. Heart in her throat, Tessa's mind became a whirl. All she could think about was this ruggedly handsome man in front of her with such beautiful brown eyes that she wanted to lose herself in them for as long as time would allow. Trembling, she accepted the cigar box and dared to open it.

Inside were the letters from Virgil Hollow to Evangeline Tinker, an eternal love that Dillon had told her transcended time. Shivers coursed down Tessa's spine. She lifted the old letters that had been lovingly kept by Dillon's ancestor since the nineteenth century, wondering if their magic might rub off on her. Beneath them, she discovered a ring.

In the center of the ring's silver setting was a piece of turquoise surrounded by diamonds. Tessa recognized the rich color of the stone—it was the one Iron Feather had handed down in his medicine pouch to Dillon. She peered closer at the ring and picked it up. Turning it over, she released a gasp.

Stamped on the silver behind the turquoise was the maker's hallmark: *Dillon*.

"You made this for me?" she whispered, astonished. She couldn't help herself—she set down the cigar box on the floor and grasped Dillon's cheeks for a kiss.

"Does that mean yes?" Lander called out impatiently from the buffet table.

Dillon stood and gazed hopefully in her eyes. When Tessa became aware that the entire buffet line had turned around and was waiting for her response, she put two and two together.

This gala wasn't simply a fundraiser for law enforcement—though Lander did put out donation boxes and badgered everyone to fork up.

This was a surprise engagement party.

Eyes wide, she was lost for words.

Dillon nudged her with a smile. He grabbed the ring from her hand and slipped it on her left finger. "Will you marry me?"

Speechless, she studied the ring's extraordinary beauty, the way it dazzled by chandelier light, and glanced at Dillon.

"Yes!" she gushed. "But only on *one* condition, Mister Iron Feather," she raised her voice so all the guests could hear her and wagged a finger. "You'd better put in electricity and running water in that dang cabin of yours."

The ballroom erupted in laughter. Dillon kissed Tessa with a twinkle in his eye. When he broke free, he took her by the left hand and closed his palm over her ring. They both felt the warmth emitted from the stone. At that moment, an owl landed on a window ledge, the glow from the chandeliers illuminating its big yellow eyes and wintry feathers.

"I can do better than that," Dillon called out to assure the crowd. "I'll build you a whole new house myself—with all the bells and whistles."

The guests cheered while Lander's staff rolled out a cart with a three-tiered cake decorated with delicate flowers. On top, the words *Congratulations on your engagement, Dillon & Tessa* were etched in the frosting.

Tessa elbowed Dillon. "Looks like Lander thought this was a sure bet," she giggled, knowing Dillon wouldn't care for the processed flour and white sugar. "Are you going to try some cake and make this official?"

To her surprise, he scooped her up in his arms, igniting more applause from the crowd. The orchestra broke into a country line dance tune and people flooded back to the dance floor between helpings from the buffet. Dillon carried Tessa and set her down in front of the cake. He traced a finger into the frosting and swallowed it, lips puckering a little at the sweetness. Then he gave Tessa a sly look, digging his finger into a heaping scoop of frosting and plopping it onto her lips.

"I'll do whatever it takes," Dillon smiled, watching Tessa laugh and lick off the frosting. "So the future Mrs. Iron Feather can keep those wonderful curves."

ALSO BY DIANE J. REED

FOR MORE IN THE IRON FEATHER BROTHERS SERIES...

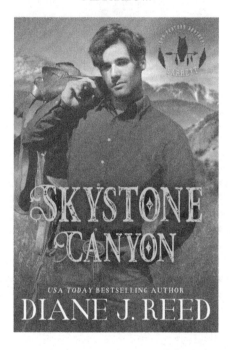

He's the toughest cowboy on patrol fighting darkness—until a rare woman reminds him of the light in his heart...

Available at your favorite retailer, and at dianejreed.com

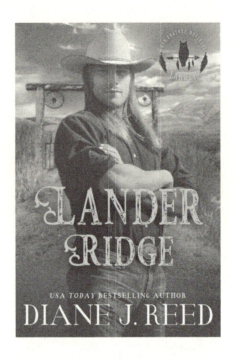

For the cowboy who wins at everything, losing his heart to the only woman who can reach his soul is the greatest risk of all…

Available at your favorite retailer, and at dianejreed.com

On a clear winter night, the Cold Moon shines a light that illuminates the past…

Available at your favorite retailer, and at dianejreed.com

THE STARLIGHT & SAGEBRUSH SERIES...

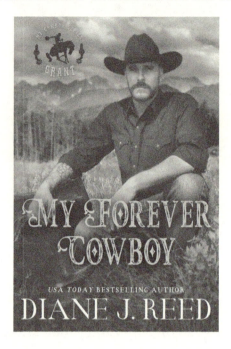

Just when you least expect it, love finds you forever...

Available at your favorite retailer, and at dianejreed.com

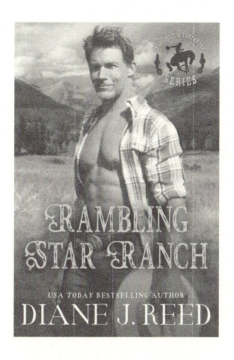

Dixon shows Tempest a whole new world where love is real on the range, second chances are worth fighting for, and only the toughest cowboys survive...

Available at your favorite retailer, and at dianejreed.com

JICARILLA APACHE LANGUAGE GLOSSARY

The fictional characters in *Turquoise Mountain* are neither full-blood Apache nor fluent speakers of the Jicarilla Apache language. In the story, however, Dillon Iron Feather acquired a few words in childhood from his mother who grew up on the Jicarilla Apache Reservation. The following Jicarilla Apache words featured in the novel are listed in alphabetical order with translations and approximate phonetic pronunciations in English. Please bear in mind that many Apache sounds do not exist in English, and Apache is a tonal language with rises, falls, nasalizations, glottal stops, and various tongue aspirations that indicate different word nuances. As a result, pronunciation accuracy can only be given justice by listening to a native Apache speaker. All Jicarilla Apache terms in *Turquoise Mountain* were derived from either native speakers or the source most trusted by the Jicarilla Apache Nation: *Dictionary of Jicarilla Apache* by Wilhelmina Phone, Maureen Olson, and Matilda Martinez published by the University of New Mexico

Press, 2007. Generous assistance was also provided by Vernon Petago, Heritage Specialist at the Jicarilla Apache Cultural Affairs Office in Dulce, New Mexico.

dáatł'iiji: (dahkl + ee + jih) **turquoise.** The accent mark indicates a long vowel with a falling tone, and the apostrophe indicates a brief stop. The "tł" consonant has a lateral tongue aspiration, which is like adding an airy "k" sound before the "l", starting from a "d" tongue position.

djił: (djih+ kl) **mountain.** The "ł" consonant has a lateral tongue aspiration, which is like adding an airy "k" sound before the "l".

dzées: (dzehs) **elk.** The accent mark indicates a long vowel with a falling tone.

goosk'aas: (goask + ahs) **cold.** The apostrophe indicates a brief stop.

hayiiłka: (hah + yeekl + kah) **sunrise.** The "ł" consonant has a lateral tongue aspiration, which is like adding an airy "k" sound before the "l".

sash: (sahsh) **bear.**

shich'oonii: (shich + oan + ee) **my friend.** The apostrophe indicates a brief stop.

yí'yee: (yih + yeh) **owl.** The accent indicates a rise in vowel tone, and the apostrophe indicates a brief stop.

ADDITIONAL TERMS

Apache: (ah + pach + ee) A Spanish word referring to the southern Athabaskan-speaking native people residing in the American Southwest and northern Mexico. To differentiate among groups, the Spanish explorers added various suffixes, such as "Apache de Jicarilla" to identify the particular band that resided in northern New Mexico and southern Colorado. Though the origin of the word Apache in Spanish is uncertain, it may be based upon the Zuni term *'a pačal*, meaning "enemies". Today, the Jicarilla Apache still use the term Apache to refer to their nation as well as the word *Dinde* (din + deh) or *Tinde* (tin + deh), meaning "The People", to refer to themselves in their own language.

Jicarilla: (hick + ah + ree + ya) Spanish word for "little basket, gourd, or cup" as well as for "little basket maker." The Spanish employed the term "Jicarilla" to describe the Apache band near Rio Chama in northern New Mexico and southern Colorado due to their extraordinary craftsmanship in weaving baskets. In addition to their artistic skills, the Spanish later learned that the Jicarilla Apache were also notoriously effective warriors.

sakwakar: (sah + kwah + kar) Ute word for turquoise.

sasquatch: (sahs + kwatch) An Anglicization of the word *sésquac*, meaning "wild man" in the language of the coastal Salish Tribe.

wapiti: (wah + pee + tee) Shawnee word for "white rump", meaning elk—a term also used by the Cree Tribe.

ABOUT THE AUTHOR

USA TODAY bestselling author Diane J. Reed writes happily ever afters with a touch of magic that make you believe in the power of love. Her stories feed the soul with outlaws, mavericks, and dreamers who have big hearts under big skies and dare to risk all for those they cherish. Because love is more than a feeling—it's the magic that changes everything.

To get the latest on new releases, sign up for Diane J. Reed's newsletter at dianejreed.com.

Made in the USA
Coppell, TX
04 August 2021